DISCARD

Best Friends Forever

Also by Kimberla Lawson Roby

THE REVEREND CURTIS BLACK SERIES

The Ultimate Betrayal
The Prodigal Son
A House Divided
The Reverend's Wife
Love, Honor, and Betray
Be Careful What You Pray For
The Best of Everything
Sin No More
Love & Lies
The Best-Kept Secret
Too Much of a Good Thing
Casting the First Stone

STANDALONE TITLES

A Christmas Prayer
The Perfect Marriage
Secret Obsession
A Deep Dark Secret
One in a Million
Changing Faces
A Taste of Reality
It's a Thin Line
Here & Now
Behind Closed Doors

Best Friends Forever

KIMBERLA LAWSON ROBY

GRAND CENTRAL
PUBLISHING

New York Boston

Grand Central Publishing
Hachette Book Group
1290 Avenue of the Americas
New York, NY 10104
HachetteBookGroup.com

Printed in the United States of America

RRD-C

First Edition: January 2016
10 9 8 7 6 5 4 3 2 1

Grand Central Publishing is a division of Hachette Book Group, Inc. The Grand Central Publishing name and logo is a trademark of Hachette Book Group, Inc.

The Hachette Speakers Bureau provides a wide range of authors for speaking events. To find out more, go to www.hachettespeakersbureau.com or call (866) 376-6591.

The publisher is not responsible for websites (or their content) that are not owned by the publisher.

Library of Congress Cataloging-in-Publication Data
Roby, Kimberla Lawson.
Best friends forever / Kimberla Lawson Roby. — First Edition.
    pages ; cm
ISBN 978-1-4555-2608-6 (hardback) — ISBN 978-1-4555-3643-6 (hardcover large print) — ISBN 978-1-61969-465-1 (audio download) 1. Domestic fiction. I. Title.
PS3568.O3189B46 2016
813'.54—dc23
                            2015030374

My Best Friends for Life

Will M. Roby, Jr.
Willie Stapleton, Jr.
Michael Stapleton
Patricia Haley-Glass
Kelli Tunson Bullard
Lori Whitaker Thurman
Janell Francine Green

Best Friends Forever

Chapter 1

Celine Richardson sat in fury as her husband walked in their bedroom. "Keith, do you know what time it is?"

"Five a.m.," he said, clearly sounding as though this was no big deal.

"And you think you can just leave the house and waltz back in here whenever you feel like it? You must be out of your mind if you think I'm going to put up with this kind of crap. I almost called the police to report you missing."

Keith pulled his short-sleeve shirt over his muscular shoulders and dropped it on the chair. "Time got away from me."

Celine folded her arms. "Where were you, Keith?"

"At a friend's. A bunch of us guys played cards and had a little too much to drink. And I fell asleep."

Celine laughed out loud. "And you think I believe that? You think I'm that naïve?"

"Believe whatever you want. That's on you."

"You have a lot of nerve staying out till the wee

hours of the morning and then acting like you're the one who's upset. How dare you."

"I'm upset because anytime a wife decides that her work is more important than her husband, she shouldn't worry one bit about where he's going...or what he's doing."

"Excuse me? So you're now staying out late and sleeping with only God knows who because you feel neglected? Please."

"I've been telling you this for months. More like a whole year. But nothing's changed. You spend all your time online doing work for your clients, and that's basically where things end with you."

"That's not true, and you know it."

"Well, actually, you're right. You spend lots of time with Kassie, but with the exception of our daughter, everything else revolves around your business. Which means there's no time for me."

"Why is it that you can spend all the time you want focusing on your career, but I can't? It took a lot of hard work for me to build up my client list, and it's completely unfair for you to ask me to give that up. Especially since I've never asked you to give up anything."

Keith was vice president of sales for a health care insurance company, and Celine had always supported him and encouraged him to excel every step of the way. So none of his complaints about her spending hours on her social media marketing business made sense. It was as if he now despised the fact that she was finally seeing some real success with her career.

She'd started her business five years ago, and she'd worked her behind off, doing everything she could not only to get it off the ground, but also to gain as much exposure as possible with both small companies and major corporations. It was the reason she now sometimes had to pass on projects or refer clients to some of her colleagues.

"Do whatever you want," he said, pulling on his pajama bottoms. "Because that's exactly what I'm doing."

Celine pulled her flowing hair around to her shoulder. "And what is that supposed to mean?"

"It's not like I stuttered. My words were very clear."

"So who exactly are you sleeping with, Keith?" she asked, ignoring his last comment.

"Look, I'm tired, and I have to be at work in three hours. So can I at least get an hour of sleep in peace? Without all these ridiculous questions?"

"You're the one who decided to stay out, so I'll ask any questions I want."

Keith sighed and got in bed, turning his back to her.

"I'm telling you now, I won't put up with this," Celine said.

Keith didn't respond.

"Are you listening to me?"

He still didn't say anything.

"Keith!" she yelled, becoming angrier.

He finally turned toward her in a huff and sat up. "What? And why are you screaming at me when you know Kassie is sleeping?"

"Because I want answers, and I want them now."

He pointed his finger at her. "I told you months and months ago that I was tired of going to bed at night with no one lying next to me. I told you how tired I was of you staying in your office until well after midnight. Work, work, and more work. That's all you've cared about for more than a year, and I finally got sick of it. I complained and tried to talk to you about it several different times, but you never took me seriously. You did what you wanted, and now I'm fine with it."

"But you know how hard it is to start your own business. Before I even decided to go forward with it, you and I talked about what it would take. We discussed all the time I'd have to spend to make it work, and you were good with that."

"Yeah, I supported you a hundred percent, but when I started to see how you had no problem talking on the phone to your friend Lauren for sometimes as much as two hours and how you never miss any of your favorite TV shows, that's when I realized how unimportant I was to you. Your priorities are totally in place, but they certainly don't include me. And don't get me started on how little we make love. Sometimes only once a month. And in case you haven't noticed, I stopped asking you to do that a long time ago."

Celine thought about everything Keith was saying, and she couldn't deny that some of his statements were true. She hadn't paid much attention to the time she spent doing other things, but now she had no choice but to acknowledge it. Nonetheless, this still didn't give him the right to break his vows to her. He wouldn't admit that he was having an affair, but no man stayed out as late as Keith had unless there was another woman involved.

"I'm sorry," she finally said. "I had no idea things were this bad between us. That you felt so neglected."

"Well, I did. But when you ignored me, I finally stopped talking about it. You acted as though I should just grow up and get over it, and I have."

"Baby, I'm sorry. I never meant to make you feel that way. But for the last five years, I've had to put my all into my business. If I hadn't, it would've failed very quickly."

"And I get that. I always did. But it's like I just told you, instead of spending some of your free time with me, you did other things. Stuff that obviously gave you a lot more satisfaction than I could."

"Do you really believe that?"

"Not only do I believe it, I'm sure of it."

"Why? Because I talked on the phone to Lauren sometimes? And I watched a few TV programs? I did those things to unwind, but never because I didn't want to be with you. And it's not like you and I haven't done things together. We've taken I don't know how many weekend trips, and we also have date nights."

"No, we *used* to take weekend trips and have date nights, but we haven't done either in over a year."

"So because you had a few unhappy months out of twelve years of marriage, you decided to find someone else?"

Keith sighed again. "This isn't about someone else. It's about you and me."

"But just tell me flat out. Are you having an affair or not?"

Keith turned his back to her again and laid his head on his pillow.

Celine wanted to ask him once more. Make him tell her what she already knew. But a part of her honestly didn't want to hear her own husband admit he was sleeping with another woman. Not when she was worried to death about something else—the lump she'd discovered in her left breast yesterday morning. She'd noticed it while in the shower, doing her monthly self-exam, but she hadn't told Keith anything about it. She hadn't told her best friend, Lauren, either, although Celine knew her silence mostly had to do with her believing it couldn't be anything serious. She also couldn't bear the thought of how their ten-year-old daughter would be affected. Along with God and Keith, Kassie was everything to Celine, and the idea of not being there for her brought Celine to tears.

But regardless of how much Celine wanted to pretend she hadn't felt anything in her breast, she knew she couldn't ignore it. Whether she wanted to or not, she had to call and make an appointment with her gynecologist. Not tomorrow or next week, but today. She needed to see Dr. McKinley as soon as possible.

Chapter 2

*C*eline's fears had haunted her all morning. When she'd called Dr. McKinley's office, she'd learned that another patient had just canceled and Celine was given that appointment. Now she was en route and trying her best to stay positive and calm. But the idea of having cancer truly terrified her. Of course, if she did have it, it wasn't like she could do anything except deal with it, but she hoped this wasn't the case.

Celine drove along in her silver Mercedes S550, praying silently. But then something dawned on her. None of this, not the luxury vehicles she and Keith both drove around in or the massive house they'd purchased a few years back, would mean anything if she didn't have her health. Not to mention, what good was any of it if she and Keith ended up in divorce court? With the way things were going, her entire life was falling apart, and it was happening pretty abruptly. Thinking negatively wasn't good, but it was hard not to. Especially when there was in fact a lump in her breast.

After another ten minutes passed, she turned into the parking lot of the medical building. It was nearly full, but after coasting through three different aisles, she finally found a spot and took it. She turned off her ignition, grabbed her shoulder bag, and got out of her vehicle. She walked a good ways, entered through the sliding glass doors, and proceeded toward a set of elevators. She pushed the button and when the elevator arrived, she stepped onto it, taking it to the fifth floor.

When the doors opened, she strolled down the carpeted hallway and went inside Dr. McKinley's office.

The twentysomething receptionist smiled. "Hi, can I help you?"

"I have a two o'clock appointment with Dr. McKinley. I'm Celine Richardson."

The receptionist checked her computer. "Are you still on Palladia Drive?"

"Yes, that's correct."

"Is Blue Cross Blue Shield still your insurance carrier?"

"Yes, it's through my husband's employer."

"Do you have a copay?"

"No, I don't."

The receptionist scrolled through a few more items. "It doesn't look like we had you sign our privacy statement last time. So, if you would, could you please sign it now?" she said, passing Celine a clipboard with a document and a pen attached to it.

"Sure."

Celine signed it and passed it back to her.

"Okay, I think that's it. You can have a seat, and someone should be coming to get you soon."

"Thanks so much."

"You're very welcome."

Celine walked toward the waiting area, where two other women were sitting, and sat down. *Family Feud* was on, and while Celine stared at the flat-screen television on the wall, trying to pay attention to it, she couldn't focus. Normally she loved watching Steve Harvey hosting her favorite game show, but right now her mind pondered three questions: Why was this happening, what had she done to deserve it, and how long did she have to live?

She knew it was crazy to be thinking so morbidly, what with the fact that she hadn't even been diagnosed with anything, but the whole idea of what might be had taken total control of her psyche. For some reason, she had a bad feeling about all of this, and it wouldn't go away.

Celine tried watching the game show again, but then she looked toward the table at her right and noticed a popular women's magazine. She shook her head when she saw that one of the featured articles was about breast cancer. What were the chances of her seeing this now? Was it a sign of things to come? *Dear God, please don't let this be happening to me.*

Lisa, Dr. McKinley's medical assistant, opened the door. "Celine?"

Celine smiled and stood up.

"So how are you today?" Lisa asked.

"Okay, I guess. How about you?"

"I'm good. Before we head into the examination room, I'll have you stop here so we can get your weight."

Celine stepped onto the scale, Lisa jotted down the numbers 1-6-0 on a small notepad, and they walked down the corridor.

"You can hang your purse right here," Lisa said, pointing toward a metal hook, "and have a seat next to the desk."

Celine sat down, and Lisa took her vitals.

"Your blood pressure is one-eighteen over seventy-eight, and your pulse is seventy-two."

"That's good to hear."

Lisa asked Celine the usual questions: Was she taking any medications, and had she had any surgeries since her last visit? Celine told her no on both counts.

"So you're here today because of a lump you found?"

"Yes. I felt it while doing a self-exam yesterday morning."

As Celine talked, Lisa typed the information into Celine's electronic chart.

"Are you having any pain?"

"No."

"Any changes in appetite?"

"No."

Lisa entered additional information and then rolled back from the desk. She stood up and pulled a pink paper gown and a white paper drape from the cupboard. "I'll leave these here, and you can undress from the waist up."

"Okay, thanks."

"It was good to see you again, and Dr. McKinley should be in shortly."

"It was good seeing you too, Lisa."

Once Celine removed her bra and sleeveless shirt, she slipped on the gown, got onto the table, and covered her knees and legs with the white paper. She sat there for thirty seconds, trying not to think about anything, but it wasn't long before she thought about Keith and everything he'd said to her this morning. Had things actually been that bad for more than a year? Had he tried talking to her on multiple occasions, but she hadn't stopped long enough to fully hear him? Had she maybe thought that just because *she* was happy, he must have been happy, too? She wasn't sure where or how they'd gone wrong, and now she wondered if they could fix their problems. In the past, she'd always made it very clear to Keith that if he ever had an affair, their marriage would be over. She'd told him that there wouldn't be any questions or discussions...only divorce proceedings. And she'd meant what she'd said with every part of her being. But now, as she sat there waiting for Dr. McKinley to come in, she found herself wishing that Keith was there with her, supporting her and telling her that if she did have cancer, they would get through this whole thing together. She was embarrassed to admit—even to herself—that she might be willing to forgive him if he ended his affair for good. It was amazing how a person's standards could change when they feared dying.

"Good afternoon," the beautiful Dr. McKinley said, walking in and shutting the door behind her. Her smile and bedside manner were as kind as always.

"Good afternoon, Doctor."

"So, I hear you felt a lump yesterday?"

"Yeah, unfortunately, I did."

Dr. McKinley sat down and clicked through a few pages on the computer. "It looks like you just had your first mammogram six months ago, and it was normal."

"I did. Right when I turned forty."

"Well, let's take a look," Dr. McKinley said, standing up and lowering the examination table. "It's your left one, right?"

Celine lay on her back. "Yes."

"Go ahead and raise your left arm over your head."

Celine did what she was asked, and Dr. McKinley kneaded her breast with the tips of her fingers around the entire circumference. "Right here?" she said when she felt something.

"Yes, that's it."

Dr. McKinley pressed the area a few times, and then she checked the center portion of Celine's breast. When she found nothing there, she pressed the area where the lump was again.

"There's definitely a lump of some kind," she said.

"Do you think it's serious?"

"It doesn't have to be, but I really think you should have another mammogram. I'll ask Lisa to get one scheduled for you. Then once you get dressed, she'll come in to give you an appointment time."

Celine didn't say anything.

"It looks like you went to our women's center last November, so is that where you'd like to go again?"

"Yes, that's fine."

Dr. McKinley looked at Celine with a somewhat reserved smile. "I know you're worried, but let's just hope for the best. Not all lumps are malignant."

"I know, and I'll try to remember that. It's very hard, though."

"Hopefully Lisa can get you scheduled pretty quickly, so we can find out what's going on. In the meantime, you take care, okay?"

"I will, and thank you, Doctor."

"You're quite welcome."

When Dr. McKinley left, Celine got dressed and waited for Lisa to come in with her appointment time. Surely a malignant tumor hadn't begun growing within the past six months; unless they'd somehow missed it when she'd had her mammogram in November. Maybe it had been too small of a growth to detect back then. She knew that was certainly possible, but deep down, she was counting on how low the odds were that she now all of a sudden had cancer.

She wondered if maybe it was time to tell Keith what was going on. But she decided it was better to wait. It was best not to tell him anything until she received her test results—and learned her fate, one way or the other.

Chapter 3

Celine sat outside her daughter's school, waiting for her to come out. Normally Kassie rode the bus home, but today Celine had decided to pick her up. It was true that Celine should have been home, working on a project for one of her clients, but she also felt this great need to spend time with her daughter. Her baby. The wonderful little girl she'd loved and cherished since conception. The daughter she'd hoped and prayed for and had been blessed with. The child she never wanted to be without.

Celine leaned her head against the headrest, thinking about her upcoming mammogram. It was scheduled for Wednesday, which was only two days from now. She hated having to deal with all this, but she knew wallowing in self-pity wasn't going to change anything. There was no doubt that whatever the answer was, she would have to accept it—whether she wanted to or not. Life was funny like that, and no one ever truly knew what would happen next. One minute, everything could seem perfect, and seconds later, it could all fall to pieces. Illness, death, financial woes, divorce—you name it and at some point, every human being was guaranteed to face two or more life-altering scenarios, let alone all the other troubles that a person could encounter. This was the very reason her mom used to say, "Enjoy your life while you can, because tomorrow isn't promised to you."

Celine missed her mother terribly, and if there was ever a time when she needed her to be here, it was now. If only she could talk to her in person, or by phone, even. Celine did still talk to her regularly, but she just wished her mother were alive and well. After being stricken with pneumonia ten years ago, she'd passed away, and for a while Celine had wondered if she would ever get over it. To be honest, she wasn't sure she could have, had it not been for the fact that she knew she needed to pull herself together for her new baby daughter. It was bad enough that her father had passed away ten years before that, but when Celine had lost her mom, it had been much more devastating. Maybe because once she and her brother, Jackson, had lost both parents, they'd felt more like orphans. It was especially traumatic for Celine because of how close she and her mother had been. She'd loved her dad with all her heart, too, but after their parents had divorced, Celine and Jackson hadn't seen their dad as much as they would have liked. He wasn't a deadbeat by any account, but seeing him only one or two days during the week and every other weekend just hadn't compared to seeing him daily. Everything had changed, and Celine and Jackson's bond with their mom had surpassed the one they'd had with their dad on so many levels.

Celine smiled when she saw Kassie walking toward the car. Celine had purposely parked near her daughter's assigned bus so that Kassie would see her right away.

Kassie opened the door and got in, smiling.

"Hi, sweetie. So how was school today?"

"Good," Kassie said, fastening her seat belt. "We learned about more animals, so we'll be ready for our field trip next week. All the kids are so excited, and so am I."

"The zoo is always fun. I loved going myself when I was a child."

"Oh, and guess what, Mom?"

"What?"

"My teacher says that I'm already reading at an eighth-grade level. And I'll only be in sixth grade this fall."

"That's wonderful, honey, and I'm so not surprised. You've been reading since you were in preschool, and I made sure to read to you before you were born."

Kassie laughed. "That's really funny, Mom. You read to me before I even got here? Do you think I heard anything?"

Now Celine laughed. Every time this subject came up, Kassie asked the same questions. "Yeah, I do. I think you heard every single word."

"Well, I sure don't remember any of it."

"I know, but it's all inside your brain somewhere," she said, looking at Kassie and smiling.

Kassie smiled back, and Celine wanted to burst into tears. She had to stay strong and upbeat, though. She couldn't let on to her daughter that something was wrong.

"Why'd you pick me up, Mom?"

"I thought we would go to the mall. You know, do something fun."

"On a Monday?"

"Yep."

"We never go shopping on Mondays. Only on Fridays and Saturdays."

"I know, but I was just in the mood for us to spend some time together."

"Oh."

"Unless you don't wanna go shopping. If not, we can head home."

"No!" Kassie hurried to say. "Let's go to the mall now."

Celine laughed. "Yeah, that's what I thought."

When they arrived, they went straight to Macy's, and Kassie picked out two summer dresses for church, two shorts sets, and a couple of cute, colorful T-shirts.

Celine repositioned all of the clothing on her left arm. "You should probably get another two or three dresses, and then we'll go up to the shoe department to get you some new sandals."

Kassie looked at her strangely. "So I can get anything I want?"

"Yep. Anything at all. And then after we leave the mall, I was thinking we could stop at that little drive-in burger place you love so much."

Kassie seemed confused, but she browsed through the dress rack anyway.

Celine wasn't confused at all. She knew she hadn't been diagnosed with anything, but there was still a chance that the worst could happen. So she'd made up her mind to treat this particular shopping trip like it was their last. Celine's new goal was to spend as much quality time with Kassie as possible, doing everything she could to make her daughter happy. What she wanted was to provide Kassie with lots of fun memories—just in case.

"I think that's all I see, Mom," Kassie said.

"Okay, then, let's go into the dressing room so you can try everything on."

As they walked through the girls' department, however, Celine's phone rang. To her surprise, it was Keith. He almost never called her on her cell phone anymore, so she wondered what was wrong.

"Go ahead and get started, sweetie," she said to Kassie and then walked a few steps away from the dressing room area. "Hello?"

"Hey, where are you?"

"At the mall."

"Oh. You and Kassie?"

"Yeah, I picked her up from school."

"I was hoping to catch you before you got home. Is she nearby?"

"No, she's in the dressing room."

"I should have called you earlier to give you the heads-up. Just in case she asks you anything about it."

"Asks me about what?"

"When she got to school this morning, she called me before she walked inside."

"Why?"

"She wanted to know why I came home so late."

"Oh yeah? And what did you tell her?"

"That I fell asleep at a friend's house by mistake. I told her I didn't realize what time it was."

"Hmmph."

"What's that supposed to mean?"

"Nothing, Keith. Nothing at all."

"Well, if she brings it up to you, I hope you'll explain it to her. Because I could tell she was upset."

"You mean lie to her the same way you did? I don't think so."

"Look. Time really did get away from me, just like I told you. I never meant to stay gone so many hours."

"Yeah, I believe that part, but you and I both know you weren't at some friend's house."

"Let's not do this. You're at the mall, and I'm still at work."

"Whatever," she said.

"I'll just see you and Kassie when I get home."

"Fine," she said, and ended the call.

If Celine hadn't heard Keith's words with her own ears, she wouldn't have believed them. He actually wanted her to support the lie he'd told both her and their daughter. Celine would never want to hurt Kassie or give her any reason to worry about anything, but she didn't want to lie to her about her father's actions. Keith was acting totally out of character, and Celine wondered when he was going to stop. He seemed so distant and uncaring and nothing like the man she'd married. She was to the point where she barely knew who he was anymore. He was different, and he was getting worse as the days went on. But regardless of how much she loved him and didn't want to live without him, she wouldn't allow him to keep going and coming as he pleased. It was bad enough that she'd tolerated his coming home so late this morning, but she wouldn't let it continue. Friend or mistress, breast cancer or not, she wouldn't be Keith's fool. He wouldn't do whatever he wanted and get away with it.

Chapter 4

*C*eline cleansed her smooth, supple face, brushed her teeth, and rinsed with mouthwash. She pulled the belt of her pink silk robe a bit tighter and walked back into the bedroom. It was only six a.m., but Keith was almost fully dressed. This was an hour earlier than usual, and Celine wondered why. He also hadn't gotten home until sometime after eight last night, claiming he'd had to work late again.

Celine attempted to make small talk. "So do you have another busy day?"

He stood in front of the dresser, tying his tie. "For the most part."

"Is there a reason for that?"

Keith frowned, but he still didn't turn to look at her. She saw his expression through the mirror.

"What do you mean?" he said.

"Is there a reason you're having to work so much overtime?"

"In case you've forgotten, I'm a VP. I have a lot of responsibility, and so do the people who report to me."

"Yeah, I realize that, but you didn't start working late every single night until about a month ago. It started all of a sudden."

Keith sighed, noticeably irritated. "I'm sorry to be the bearer of bad news, but I don't get to decide when there's going to be a lot of work and when there isn't. Right now, we have a lot going on, and there's nothing I can do about it."

Celine didn't bother bringing up the fact that he'd stayed out Sunday night and hadn't come home until yesterday morning. She didn't mention how his late-night-into-the-morning escapade had nothing to do with his job.

Instead, she took a different approach. "What is it I need to do, Keith? What will it take for us to make things right with our marriage?"

"I really need to get going," he said. "Maybe we can discuss it another time, though."

"So you're just going to walk out? Leave right in the middle of our conversation?"

"I don't see what there is to talk about. When I wanted to talk months ago, you were too busy."

"I never tried to ignore you intentionally. I admit that I was pretty caught up with my work, but when you know better, you can do better. I'm sorry if you felt neglected, and I'm sorry I didn't hear you when you were trying to make me aware of it."

Keith pulled on his blazer in silence.

"Can I meet you for lunch?" she asked. "Can we go somewhere and talk then?"

"My day is too full for that."

"What about dinner? Can't you leave work early just this one time?".

"No, I can't."

"Even if it has to be a late dinner, Lauren won't mind watching Kassie. Actually, we could just have Kassie spend the night with Lauren, which she loves to do anyway. And Lauren can just take her to school in the morning."

"I have a lot of work to do, Celine. What part of that don't you understand?"

"Why are you so angry? Why are you doing this?"

Keith shook his head, walked over to the chair, and picked up his briefcase. "I have to go."

Celine folded her arms. "Who is she, Keith?"

This time he stopped and stared at her with no emotion, and his silence was chilling. He hadn't answered her one way or the other, but the look on his face told her that he wasn't planning to deny her accusation. He hadn't done so yesterday, either, but there was something different about the way he looked at her now, almost as if he didn't have the nerve to say it out loud, yet he wanted her to know the truth. Although maybe she was making more out of this than it actually was. Maybe he was simply staying out late so she would *think* he was messing around. Maybe this was some unorthodox way of trying to pay her back for not spending any quality time with him. Or maybe he was simply doing this to get her attention so she could see how serious things were.

Every bit of that could be true, but Celine knew in

her heart that it wasn't. He was acting far too differently, and it had started pretty suddenly. It was as if Keith had awakened one day last month and decided he was a free man, as though he didn't have a wife or a child to answer to.

"Look, Keith," she said. "Marriages have problems. Remember when your parents first joined that church they go to? And they told us that if we didn't join, too, they couldn't have anything to do with us? We haven't seen your parents in years, and I was there for you through all of that. Even when you were so hurt you walked around not saying anything to me. But like I said, marriages have problems, and problems can be worked on. So, if you're willing, I'd like to find a good counselor for us to talk to."

"I think our situation is beyond that point."

"You can't be serious. Not after all this time we've been together. Not with the way I've always loved you and the way you claimed you always loved me."

"I do love you," he said. "But over the last year, my feelings really changed. I lost some of that love. I do love you as the mother of my child, but I don't feel the way I did before. I'm sorry."

Celine looked at him, not knowing what to say. She considered telling him about the mammogram appointment she had scheduled for tomorrow. And she would have, except before she could open her mouth, he said, "See you later," and walked out of the bedroom.

Celine went over to the window, watching him back out of the driveway, and then she sat on the side of the bed, heartbroken. She just couldn't understand how this had happened and why it was going on now.

She broke into tears, but right when she did, Kassie walked into her room. She still had on her cute little pajamas, but she looked sad.

Kassie stood directly in front of her. "Mom, why are you crying?"

Celine quickly wiped her face with both hands, trying to appear as though nothing were wrong. "Everything's fine, honey."

"You don't look fine. You look sad, and so am I."

"Sit down, sweetie," Celine said. "Why are you sad?"

"Because you and Daddy must be mad at each other again."

"Why would you think that?"

"Because you argue all the time. You're always mad at each other."

"Honey, it's nothing like that."

"Why didn't Daddy come home on Sunday night?" she asked, looking directly into her mother's eyes.

Celine was shocked by the things Kassie was saying. She'd had no idea that Kassie was overhearing their arguments. Although, why wouldn't she when there had definitely been times when their voices were louder than normal?

"Sweetheart," Celine said, "your dad is very busy with work, and it's taking up a lot of his time. But it won't always be this way, okay?"

"But yesterday when I called him from school, he told me that he was at a friend's house."

Celine swallowed hard, trying to think of what to say next. She wasn't prepared for the comments Kassie was making or the questions she was asking.

"He fell asleep, but you know your dad has never done anything like this before, right?" Celine's own words made her sick to her stomach. She hated defending Keith to their daughter, when she knew in her gut he hadn't just fallen asleep at some *friend's* house. But she also didn't have the heart to say anything that would make Kassie worry more than she already was.

"Come here," Celine said, hugging her.

Kassie laid her head against her mother's chest, and silent tears rolled down Celine's face. Celine squeezed Kassie tighter and prayed she didn't have breast cancer. And the more she thought about it, maybe she didn't. Based on a bit more research that she'd done online last night, thousands of women discovered lumps all the time, and actually, when she'd had her first mammogram last year, she'd been told that she had lumpy breasts. So maybe she'd gotten herself all worked up for nothing. There was a chance that she'd prematurely decided the worst when it was best to wait and see what happened.

Celine held her daughter and hoped she was right. She prayed that when she left the women's center tomorrow, all would be well, and that none of this had been more than a false alarm. She had to believe this for her own sake and for the sake of her daughter. Otherwise, she wasn't sure how she'd make it through the day.

Chapter 5

*C*eline sat outside the women's center meditating and praying. She was a whole half hour early, but she was glad she'd arrived when she had so she could try to settle her nerves. From the time she'd gotten up this morning, a thousand thoughts had circulated her mind, and she'd barely been able to keep her composure. She'd even come close to telling Keith about her appointment and asking him to call in to work so he could take her, but she'd decided it was best to deal with this on her own. She'd also considered calling her best friend, Lauren, last night, this morning, and again only a few minutes ago. But why worry anyone before she knew her results? Why upset those who cared about her when there was likely nothing to be concerned about?

Celine closed her eyes, listening to one of her favorite gospel songs, "It's Working" by William Murphy. When it finished playing on her iPod, she selected another one of her favorites, "Grateful" by Hezekiah

Walker. As usual, both songs brought tears to her eyes, and because of the joy they gave her, she played each of them a second time. Then she prayed again, took a deep breath, and stepped out of her car. When she walked inside the women's center, she waited behind another patient who was already in line.

After Celine checked in for her appointment, one of the receptionists met her at the door leading to the waiting room and took her back to the dressing area. The room was lined with a wall of wooden lockers.

"You'll only need to remove your top and bra, and if you have on deodorant you can remove it with one of the packaged wipes over there," the receptionist said, pointing to a beautifully decorated basket. "You can then slip on the robe I have here and take a seat in the waiting area around the corner. There's water and tea available as well."

"Thank you so much," Celine told her, and the receptionist left.

Celine removed her clothing from the waist up, the same as she had two days ago at Dr. McKinley's office, and slipped on a pink cotton wraparound robe. She also took off the diamond heart necklace Keith had given her two years ago for her birthday, and while she knew she didn't need to, she removed her watch as well. Normally she wore a bracelet or two daily and a silver ring on her right hand, but today she only wore her wedding solitaire—a ring that had symbolized her happy marriage for twelve years. But now she and Keith seemed worlds apart. At least, this was how Keith had been acting. Celine couldn't fathom the idea of his sleeping around with another woman, but just as she'd been thinking the last few days, she wasn't naïve. All the signs were in place, and he hadn't denied her accusations.

Celine walked into the waiting area and smiled at the only woman sitting there. The woman smiled back and it was obvious that, for whatever reason, they were both nervous and anxious to get their testing over with. The TV channel was set on HGTV and though Celine tried to watch it, she couldn't focus on it the way she normally did. Then, when the other patient was called back by a nurse, Celine found herself worrying about the lump in her breast, along with her troubled marriage.

Only minutes later, a different nurse came to get Celine and they took a seat in an office.

"How are you today?" the nurse asked.

"I could be better, but I won't complain." Celine forced a smile.

"Well, I'm Judith, and I'll be doing your mammogram today. But first, I need to ask you a few questions," she said, pulling out a sheet of paper with an illustration of a breast on it and circling the area in question. "Is this the area your doctor found the lump in?"

"Yes. I found it on Sunday, and she confirmed it two days ago."

"It's always good to hear that someone really is doing self-exams. So many more lives could be saved if all women did," Judith said. "Some women won't even have a mammogram done at all, even though they're well past forty."

"I know a couple of women myself who don't see a reason to get one, and it's very sad."

"I agree. Now, I do have your family history here from last time, but has anything changed?"

"No. None of my relatives were ever diagnosed with breast cancer."

Judith asked her a few more questions and then led her into the imaging room. Getting a mammogram wasn't excruciating, but when the compression plate clamped down on Celine's breast, she definitely felt it. Judith took multiple images, and it was a bit uncomfortable each time. Still, getting either a yearly screening or a diagnostic mammogram, which is what Celine was having now, was well worth it and very necessary.

When her testing was complete, Judith escorted her back to the waiting area. "You can have a seat, but please don't get dressed, because once the radiologist takes a look, he'll let us know if he has everything or if you'll need additional testing."

"Okay, thanks," Celine said.

Celine flipped through a few magazines, but soon she became too nervous to concentrate. So she got up and walked around the room. Then to make matters worse, Judith called her back into her office, letting Celine know that the radiologist wanted her to have an ultrasound. Celine knew this couldn't be good. She'd done enough research to know that when an ultrasound was ordered, the radiologist either needed a much better image or he didn't like what he saw from the mammogram results and wanted to confirm his opinion.

"One of our ultrasound technicians will come get you shortly. And if you'd like to wait for those results as well, you're welcome to do so, or we can call you."

"I think I'll wait."

"Sounds good."

The ultrasound testing hadn't taken long, and now Celine sat in the waiting area again. She did more praying. She was ashamed to say that she hadn't prayed this much in years. Now she wished she had, because it was never good to wait until something was wrong before spending adequate time with God. It was much better to thank Him daily for watching over you and protecting you, and sadly, Celine had become a little lax in that area. She knew God's will would be done either way, but from now on, she wouldn't go days without praying. Her mom used to say, "We have to stay prayed up at all times," and Celine was now in a place where she took those words seriously.

Celine waited as patiently as possible, still hoping and praying for the best. But then Judith called her back to her office again.

"Well, the good news is that we finally have all the images we need, but the not-so-good news is that you definitely have a tumor of some kind. I can't give you full details, but once the radiologist compiles a final report, he'll be sending it over to Dr. McKinley."

Celine could barely breathe, but she tried not to show how afraid she was. "I know every case is different, but can you tell me what the next steps might be?"

"Chances are, Dr. McKinley will refer you to a breast surgeon who will consult with you and perform a biopsy."

Celine's heart beat faster and faster, and tears filled her eyes.

Judith rested her hand on top of Celine's. "I'm really sorry I don't have better news, but please try to stay positive. It's always best to wait and hear what your specialist has to say."

Celine hoped—desperately—that Judith would continue her comments with something like "We still don't know if it's cancer or not." But she didn't, and Celine wondered if she knew more than what she was telling her. Maybe Judith already knew the tumor wasn't benign. Celine wanted to ask her, but she didn't want to place her in an awkward position. So instead, Celine thanked her and went to get dressed.

She tried to stay positive the way Judith had advised her, but she couldn't. However, when she went outside and got in her car, she made a decision. She would deal head-on with whatever the diagnosis was, and tonight, she would tell Keith everything. She would also tell Lauren, because Celine was finally at a point where she needed strong moral support and constant encouragement. As much as she hated to burden anyone, she couldn't do this alone. She just didn't have the strength to, or even the will, for that matter.

Chapter 6

It was six p.m., and Celine and Kassie were having dinner. This morning, Celine had planned to cook something, but after receiving the news about her test results, she hadn't felt up to it. Kassie didn't mind, of course, not with her loving Chinese food as much as she did. Celine had also tried calling Keith three times, but he hadn't answered, and this added to her sadness. She was hurt, afraid, and starting to get angry, but she did all she could not to display her emotions in front of her daughter.

"Everyone is so excited about Delia's birthday sleepover on Friday," Kassie said, blowing the egg drop soup on her spoon, trying to cool it down before eating it.

"I'm sure. Sleepovers are always fun."

"I know, and I'm just glad Delia is the one having it so I can get to go."

Celine smiled because while Kassie never did much complaining, she wasn't always happy about the fact that Celine rarely allowed her to spend the night with friends. To be honest, the only reason Celine was okay with Kassie staying at Delia's was because Celine was friends with Delia's mom. Celine had known Sarah for a long time, and she knew Kassie and the other girls would be safe.

"When are we going to get Delia's gift?" Kassie asked.

"Tomorrow when you get out of school. I guess we should have thought more about it when we were at the mall the other day."

"I know, but I was too busy picking out my own stuff. It was really fun, and I hope we can do it again real soon."

"I'm sure you do," Celine said, laughing. "I'm glad you had a great time, though, and so did I."

"When is Daddy coming home?" Kassie asked with no warning.

"I'm sure he'll be here soon. He's probably working late again."

"Is that who you were calling?" she wanted to know.

"Yes, but he didn't answer."

"Do you want me to call him from my phone? He always answers when I call him."

Celine felt like a fool but said, "No, that's okay. I'll just try him later."

"I really wish Daddy would start back having dinner with us again," Kassie said. "We used to have dinner together all the time, but now it's only you and me. Daddy never eats with us."

"I'm really sorry about that, sweetie" was all Celine said, because she couldn't think of anything else to say without lying.

34

"I miss him, Mom."

"I know, but it'll get better."

Kassie ate her food in silence, and so did Celine. Worrying her was one thing, but upsetting Kassie was another, and Keith should have been ashamed of himself.

When Celine and Kassie finished eating, Celine said, "So do you have any more homework to do?"

"No, I finished it all before dinner."

"Well, I'm going to clean up, and I want you to go upstairs to read for a while."

"Okay," Kassie said in a cheerful tone, already lifting her plate and utensils from the table to take into the kitchen.

Celine smiled because she loved the fact that her daughter enjoyed reading as much as she did. It was one of the reasons Kassie was such a great student. She read and understood things very quickly, regardless of what subject she was studying, and Celine and Keith had always been very happy about that.

As soon as Kassie went up to her room, Celine grabbed her cell phone and stepped outside the back door to the patio. Kassie's bedroom faced the front of the house, so Celine knew she wouldn't be able to hear her conversation.

Celine sat down at the patio table and called Lauren.

"Hey, girl, how are you?" Lauren said.

"Not so good. I was going to call you earlier, but I needed to pull myself together first."

"Why? What's wrong?"

"On Sunday, I felt a lump in my left breast, so the next day I went to the doctor. She then had me go get a mammogram today. I also had an ultrasound, and it confirmed that I have a tumor."

"Oh my, and you're just now telling me about this?"

"I knew you wouldn't be happy about that, and I'm sorry. But I just didn't want to talk about it until I knew more. I was so hoping it was maybe just a cyst or something benign."

"Are they saying it's cancerous?"

"No, but I really believe it is."

"Why?"

"It's just a feeling I have."

"Well, we're not claiming that, right? We're simply not gonna think that way."

"No, but I can't ignore the possibility, Lauren. When I left the women's center, I decided right then and there that I would deal with whatever I have to. It's not like I have a choice, anyway."

"I hear you, and I understand, but I'm gonna pray for only good news. Have you spoken to your doctor again?"

"Yes, and I'm already scheduled to see a breast surgeon on Friday."

"Keith is going with you, right? And how is he taking all this?"

Celine slightly paused and then said, "He's upset but hoping for the best." She hated lying about anything to anyone, but she still wasn't ready to tell Lauren about her problems with Keith.

"Do you think you should call Pastor Black?" Lauren said, referring to the pastor of their church, Deliverance Outreach.

"Not yet. Maybe after I see the specialist."

"I think you should. We have a large membership at Deliverance, but you know Pastor Black is very good about talking to his members. And he certainly prays for them."

"I'll think about it, and thanks so much for listening. And especially for praying, because right now, I need all the prayers I can get."

"Of course, and I'll call to check on you tomorrow."

"Thanks again."

"Love you, girl."

"Love you, too."

Celine pressed the End button on her phone. She wasn't sure why, but for some reason she thought back to the very day she and Lauren had become best friends. Celine's parents had taken her and her brother, Jackson, to a local 4-H fair, and Lauren's parents had brought her there the same afternoon. Of course, as soon as Jackson had spied two of his close friends, boys from the neighborhood, he'd begged his and Celine's parents to let him walk around and get on rides with them. Needless to say, this had left Celine without another child to ride with. That is, until she'd found herself standing in the merry-go-round line with another eight-year-old girl who didn't have anyone to ride with, either. Lauren had quickly struck up a conversation with Celine and not only had they ridden the merry-go-round together, they'd also gotten on every other ride side by side. They'd become fast friends and ultimately the best of friends, and they'd remained that way ever since. Then, when the two of them had turned twelve, Lauren's parents had moved only two blocks away from Celine's house, and they'd soon become inseparable. They'd even gone to the same junior high and high schools and had roomed together in college. They were sisters in every sense of the word, and they'd always been there for each other—through good times and not-so-great times. They also shared all their personal business with each other, and while Celine was ashamed to tell Lauren about her problems with Keith, she knew somewhere down the road, she wouldn't be able to help it. She would eventually have to tell the one person she could trust with her life—the one person she could depend on no matter how bad things got. It was the reason Celine loved Lauren with all her heart, and she would do anything for her as well.

Celine dialed Keith's cell again. There was still no answer, so she tried the direct line to his office, but he didn't answer that, either. Celine sighed and wondered where he was. She wondered why he was doing this to her. Yes, he'd explained how neglected and unloved he'd felt, but why hadn't he sat her down and been clear about how unhappy he was? It was true that he'd complained a few times, but it hadn't seemed as though he was to the point of wanting to see someone else. They'd even argued quite a bit lately, but weren't married people supposed to communicate with each other a lot better than that? Weren't they supposed to share the good, the bad, and everything in between? Didn't they have an obligation to do all they could to save their marriage? Otherwise, what good were the vows that they'd taken before God and others?

Normally, Celine wouldn't take the idea of infidelity so lightly—believing it was happening, yet doing nothing about it except sitting back, hoping it would end—but with all that she was dealing with relating to her tumor, she just didn't have that kind of fight in her right now. She didn't want to argue with Keith any more than she already was. She also didn't want to spend her time demanding that he tell her who he was seeing or playing private investigator. Saving her life was much more important. As it was, she'd already asked him who he was seeing, and he hadn't replied. Even a child knew that when a person didn't respond to a question, the answer wasn't encouraging, and it wouldn't be a happy one.

Celine went back into the house and straightened up the kitchen. Her mind switched from one thing to another, but soon she thought about her parents. Oh, how she wished they were here. Celine's parents had gotten divorced when she and Jackson were children—Celine had been ten, the same age Kassie was now, and Jackson nine, but until the day her father had died, Celine had never stopped wanting them to get back together. Jackson had seemed to deal with their parents' separation and divorce much better than she had. But to be honest, Celine had never truly gotten over it.

Now Celine thought about calling Jackson, who'd lived in Atlanta for the last nine years. He would certainly want to know what was going on, but she just couldn't tell him yet; not until she had results from the biopsy. Like Lauren, he wouldn't be happy to be learning everything after the fact, but she believed it was best not to worry him until it was necessary.

It was close to midnight. Celine had tucked Kassie in long ago, and she was now preparing to get into bed herself—until she heard Keith coming inside the house. In a matter of minutes, he walked upstairs and into their bedroom.

She stood, facing him. "Keith, didn't you see all my phone calls?"

"Yeah, I did."

"Then why didn't you call me back?"

"I was busy working, and then I was too tired on the way home. I also figured you were asleep by now."

"Working? Till close to midnight?"

"I told you this is a busy time for us. Plus, it wasn't like I was at the office this late. Some of the guys and I went and had a late dinner and before I knew it, it was after eleven."

"And you saw no reason to call me? You still think you can come in here whenever you want?"

"I told you I was working."

"You're such a liar."

"Believe what you want," he said, and then went into the closet, undressed himself, and walked back over to the bed. He got in, pulled the covers up to his neck, and turned his back to Celine.

Celine got in bed, too, but sat against her pillows. "I'm really at my wit's end, Keith, and I want the truth. At first I didn't, but I'm tired of being disrespected this way."

"Look," he said. "I'm tired, and I'm not doing this with you tonight."

"This is *exactly* when we're doing it, whether you want to or not."

Keith got up in a violent manner. "Didn't I tell you I'm tired?"

"Then you should've brought your behind home a lot earlier. So tired or not, we're talking about this now."

Keith snatched his pillow from the bed. "You can talk all you want—to yourself. Because I'm done," he said, storming out of the room. Seconds later, Celine heard him shut the door to one of the guest bedrooms.

She sat in bed, wanting to cry but refusing to do so. None of this seemed real. Her spirit had never been lower or her faith this weak, and she wasn't sure how she was going to get through it—her potential illness or the breakdown of her marriage. Right now, she just didn't know anything.

Chapter 7

Celine sat up on the examination table. Dr. Jones, her breast surgeon, had just performed an exam and reviewed her mammogram and ultrasound reports. Dr. McKinley had told her that Dr. Jones was one of the best in the region, and that he was also certified in oncology.

"We won't be positively sure about your final diagnosis until we do a biopsy, so I'd really like to get that done right away."

Celine nodded in agreement.

"What I can tell you today, however, is that your tumor is three centimeters, and whether it's benign or malignant, it will need to be removed."

Celine suddenly wished Keith were there with her. It was strange how even though he was treating her like an unwanted child, it was him she wanted to lean on. A part of her also wished she'd asked Lauren to come, and the only reason she hadn't was because she knew Lauren would question the reason Keith wasn't going with her instead. Celine wanted to tell her, but she was still too humiliated to admit any of what Keith was up to.

"So how soon do you think you can do the biopsy?" she asked.

Dr. Jones sat in front of the computer. "Well, since Monday is a holiday, I'm sure we can get you scheduled for Tuesday morning."

Celine didn't say anything, but with everything that was going on, she hadn't thought much at all about Memorial Day. Since the first year she and Keith were married, they'd celebrated every holiday, and they almost always had huge cookouts for Memorial Day and the Fourth of July. Sometimes they cooked out for Labor Day, too.

Dr. Jones typed a couple of notes and then rolled his chair around so that he was facing Celine again. "I'm really sorry you're having to go through this, but the good news is that we're already moving forward with finding out everything we can. Then, if it becomes necessary, we can begin treating you as soon as possible."

"I agree, but I have to say, Doctor...this has really caught me off guard."

"I'm sure it has, because this kind of thing is never easy. Not for anyone."

"Dr. McKinley spoke very highly of you, so I appreciate your seeing me so quickly."

"I'm glad we could get you in today," he said, standing up. "I'll let you get dressed, and after that, my nurse will be in to tell you more about the biopsy procedure. She'll also let you know the date and time.

Oh, and just so you know, I'll be doing a needle biopsy versus a surgical one."

"Is there a reason? I'm only asking because I read online that surgical biopsies are a lot more reliable than the needle versions."

"Yes, that's true, but based on your mammogram and ultrasound reports, I think a needle biopsy will give us a pretty conclusive diagnosis."

Celine heard his words, and now she couldn't help asking the one question she'd been wanting to ask for the last few minutes. "So, if you had to give an expert opinion today, based solely on what you've seen so far, what would it be?"

"There's no way to be sure until we have your biopsy results, but I don't believe this is a benign situation."

Celine's chest tightened, and her throat felt restricted. Dr. Jones hadn't said the words outright, but he was already prepared to find cancer. He didn't know exact details per se, but he believed she had a malignant tumor and he was doing the biopsy as soon as possible to confirm it.

Dr. Jones patted Celine's left shoulder, and she thought about the way Judith had rested her hand on top of hers at the women's center. Celine was very blessed to have such compassionate people helping her through this trying process.

"If you don't have any other questions," Dr. Jones said, "please try to have a great holiday and I'll see you next week."

"I think I'm good for now, and thanks again, Doctor."

When Dr. Jones closed the door behind him, Celine had to will herself to get dressed. Her mind, body, and soul were numb. Of course, she found herself thinking about Keith again, and then Kassie. Her baby. What in the world would Kassie do if something happened to Celine? She would still have her father, but with the way Keith was acting, who was to say he'd be there for his daughter the way he needed to? Life for Celine had become an instant nightmare, and it was all too much to bear. From this day on, she knew nothing would ever be the same again.

Chapter 8

*C*eline had dropped Kassie off at her sleep-over, and now she was ringing Lauren's doorbell. After Celine had left her doctor's appointment, she'd called Lauren at work and told her she was coming by this evening. Lauren had wanted to know what the doctor said, but Celine had told her she would explain everything when she saw her. It was then that Lauren had gotten quiet, which meant she already understood that the news wasn't good.

Lauren opened the front door to her condo, and she and Celine hugged for longer than usual. Lauren finally shut the door, and they went down the hall and into Lauren's den.

Celine dropped her purse onto a red leather chair, and she and Lauren sat on the matching sofa.

"So what happened?" Lauren asked, and Celine noticed how perfectly cut Lauren's hair was. Her new style was short and asymmetrical, and she looked like a forty-year-old supermodel.

"Dr. Jones thinks that I have cancer. He still needs to do a biopsy to find out for sure, but he seemed pretty positive."

Lauren shook her head with sadness. "I was so hoping that wouldn't be the case."

"Yeah, so was I, but ever since I felt the lump on Sunday, I've had a bad feeling about it. Somehow I knew this would be the result."

"This really breaks my heart, girl, but we're going to fight it until the end," Lauren said matter-of-factly. "You're going to be fine, and we're not going to consider anything different."

"I want to believe that. Really, I do. But I've never felt more downtrodden or weak in my life. Normally I can see the positive in everything. I'm the one who sees the glass as being half-full and not half-empty. But not with this. I've been thinking of the worst possible outcomes all week long."

"But that's so unlike you."

"I know, but maybe it's because I've never had a life-threatening illness. It's one thing to pray and believe the best for others, but it's something totally different when it's about you."

"That might be true, but you've got to keep your head up and know that you're going to be healed. From this moment on, you've got to meditate on Matthew nine, twenty-two, which says, "Daughter, be encouraged! Your faith has made you well." You have to keep your faith strong and rid yourself of doubt. It's the only way you can beat this."

Tears streamed down both sides of Celine's face. Lauren scooted closer to her and hugged her again.

"It really is going to be okay," Lauren assured her. "I know it doesn't feel like that now, but it will be."

Celine sniffled and wiped her eyes.

Lauren stood up. "Let me get you some tissue."

Celine tried to calm herself down, and while she was definitely upset about what Dr. Jones had told her, she was mostly sad because of how terrible things were between her and Keith. Actually, this was the real reason she had such a woe-is-me attitude about her medical situation. She was so broken that she didn't have the strength to fight the way Lauren was suggesting. She'd always been a strong, independent woman, but not now. Not with her husband staying out late every night and making it clear that he no longer wanted her. He hadn't told her this, but his actions said everything.

Lauren walked back into the den, passed Celine the Kleenex, and sat back down. "So when are you having the biopsy? Has it been scheduled yet?"

"Yes, for Tuesday. Which is four long days from now."

"Will they need to put you under?"

"No, Dr. Jones is doing it right in his office. He'll be taking a sample of the tumor by needle."

"Well, I know Keith will be with you, but I want you to call me as soon as you're settled in back at home."

"I will."

Lauren rested her right arm across the back of the sofa. "This is really turning out to be a tough year."

"Yeah, tell me about it. So has David finally stopped calling?"

Lauren pursed her lips together. "As a matter of fact, he has, but only because I blocked his number. I did it on both my home phone and my cell."

"I still can't get over what he did. It just wasn't like him. He seemed like such a great guy."

"Actually, he seemed perfect, and maybe that's what the problem was. He was putting on like he was the ideal person, but he couldn't keep up the facade."

"Well, he put up a really good one, and he did it the whole two years you were dating."

"I know, and that's why I was so devastated. I loved him, and I thought we would get married and be together forever."

Celine wiped her nose. "It just doesn't make sense. I remember when he first started talking to you about marriage."

"Yeah, but it just goes to show that if a man wants to be unfaithful, he'll do it no matter what. He can love you, be attracted to you, and still feel like he needs more. On the other hand, there are some men who make it a point to be faithful to their wives until death. And don't get me wrong, there are just as many disloyal women out here, too. Some women don't feel right unless they're sleeping around town."

"I don't get any of it. Even when I dated men who I never wanted to marry, I didn't mess around on them," Celine said. "Monogamy has always been very important to me."

"I feel the same way, and that's the reason I won't put up with that. I won't tolerate that from any man."

Celine thought about Keith and how she hadn't confronted him nearly the way she should have. But it was like she'd been thinking on Wednesday, this tumor issue had weakened her personality. She didn't like it, and although she wouldn't admit it out loud, the reason she was acting this way was because she didn't want to push Keith and cause him to leave her. She knew her thinking was crazy, spineless, and confusing, even, but she didn't want to struggle with cancer all alone. She didn't want to force Kassie to be without her father, the man she loved so dearly.

"I don't blame you" was all Celine said.

"I do want to thank you again, though," Lauren told her. "You know, for standing by me the way you did. Through all my pain and tears. It was the hardest thing I've ever been through."

"I know, but it's like my mom always used to say, 'For everything bad, something good always comes out of it.'"

"Isn't that the truth? And for me, it was my level of strength. I've never been stronger than I am now, and it's all because of what David did to me. The same will hold true for you, too. On Tuesday, you'll find out what's what, you'll go through whatever it takes to get past it, and you'll be stronger than ever."

"I hope so."

"You will. Just wait and see. And hey, have you eaten?"

"No. I don't really have an appetite."

"Well, I'm getting a little hungry, unless you and Keith already have dinner plans."

"No, he's going out with some of his coworkers," she lied.

Lauren raised her eyebrows. "After hearing what your doctor said this afternoon, he still went out somewhere?"

Celine pretended she was okay with that. "Please. I was fine, and life goes on. Plus, he knew I wanted to come talk to you about my appointment," she said, making things up as she went along. "He even offered to take Kassie over to her friend's house, but I really wanted to do it myself. I don't want things changing for her any more than they have to."

The part about Kassie was true, but sadly, Keith hadn't even come home from work, and he also hadn't returned any of Celine's calls. He was only God knew where, and Celine was certainly the least of his worries.

Lauren didn't say anything else about Keith, but it was obvious how stunned she still was about his going out with coworkers when there was a chance his wife was very ill. Of course, Keith didn't know about any of it, let alone Celine's diagnostic results or her visit to a breast surgeon. For this reason, Celine changed the subject altogether.

"So what are you doing for Memorial Day? I hadn't even thought about it until Dr. Jones mentioned it earlier."

"I don't know. Normally I come to your house," she said, and they both laughed.

"Well, I'm not sure I'll feel like cooking or celebrating, but you can still come by if you want. We'll just pick up some food from a restaurant."

"Fine with me, and speaking of food," Lauren said, scooting to the edge of the sofa, "I'm ready to order something now. What about a pizza?"

"Sounds good to me."

"I know you're not hungry, but you really should eat something," Lauren said, leaving the room so she could grab her purse.

Celine followed her, but mostly she thought about Keith again. She wondered where he was and whether he'd be home before morning.

Chapter 9

As soon as Celine heard Keith pulling into the driveway, she got out of bed, slipped on her robe without tying it, and rushed down the stairs. It was four a.m., and she hadn't slept a wink, yet Keith was just bringing his no-good behind home. Celine couldn't remember ever being more furious and hurt all at the same time, and she'd had about as much of this as she could take.

Keith strolled into the kitchen, and before he could close the door behind him, Celine went off.

"You must think I'm stupid! Where in the world have you been, Keith? Does that whore have you that caught up?"

He dropped his key fob on the island, rolling his eyes with irritation.

"Wait a minute. I know you're not rolling your eyes at me. Not when you're the one who just walked in here."

Keith looked at her as though he didn't understand English. He seemed unmoved by all that she was saying.

"What's wrong with you? What is it that I've done so terribly for you to treat me like this?"

"I knew I should have stayed where I was. I shouldn't have come back here until tomorrow night."

"Why are you doing this?"

"What?"

"Disrespecting me, our marriage, and our daughter."

"Oh, please," he said, scrunching his forehead. "Stop trying to make this about Kassie."

"Well, how long do you think we can go on like this, Keith? Huh?"

"Actually, I don't."

"Meaning what?"

"You and I need time apart."

Celine swallowed the massive lump in her throat. "What are you talking about?"

"Things are really bad between us. They're so bad, there's no way we can work them out while living under the same roof."

"That's the craziest thing I've ever heard. How is separating going to help anything?"

Keith leaned against the island. "I need time away so I can think."

"Wow," she said, laughing. "Where is all this coming from? Did that whore of yours give you some sort of ultimatum? What is this exactly?"

"I really think my moving out would be best."

"What about counseling? I just asked you about that a few days ago."

"And I told you then that I think we're beyond all

that. Plus, I have no desire to go telling my business to some stranger."

"Really? But you think moving out so you can *think* might fix everything?"

"It might," he said, and Celine wanted to slap that blasé look off his face. He glared at her like she was a nonentity—as though she were someone he barely knew and couldn't care less about.

"That trick you're sleeping with has turned you into a fool."

"Celine, please. This isn't about anyone else. I've told you before, this is about you and me. How totally disconnected we are."

"Yeah, but there's still someone else."

"I'm really tired," he said.

"I'm sure you are."

"I'm going upstairs."

"Wait," she said.

Keith frowned. "What is it?"

"I have a tumor."

"Where?" he said, sounding as though he didn't believe her.

"In my breast, and the doctor thinks it's cancerous."

"How long have you known this?"

"I noticed a lump on Sunday. I had tests on Wednesday, and I saw a breast surgeon yesterday afternoon."

Keith's face softened. "Wow. Well, I'm really sorry to hear that."

Celine didn't say anything.

"So when will they know for sure if it's cancer or not?"

"My doctor is doing a biopsy on Tuesday."

"Oh," he said, sounding relieved. "Then I think you should just wait and see what happens, because it's not like you're having any pain or anything, are you?"

"No, but you don't have to have pain to have cancer, and my doctor believes it's malignant."

"I'm sure you'll be fine."

"That's my prayer, but I also hope you understand why I need you to be here for me right now. I need your support. Especially if I really do have cancer, because I'll then need surgery and probably chemo or radiation. There's a chance I might need both. Kassie will need you a whole lot more, too."

"I think you're jumping the gun on this a little bit."

"I don't think so, and if you don't mind, I'd really like you to go with me to my appointment on Tuesday."

"I wish you'd told me a lot earlier. That way I could've asked my secretary to reschedule my Tuesday morning meetings."

"I did try to tell you earlier. I called you several times, but you never answered or called me back, remember?"

"Well, that's beside the point. I can't just go missing important meetings without giving notice."

"So you're a VP, and you're telling me that your colleagues won't understand that you need to take your wife to the doctor? Your wife who might have cancer?"

"I don't think I can, but I'll see what I can do."

Celine shook her head. "Gosh, Keith. Not in a million years."

"What?"

"Not in a million lifetimes would I have thought you'd have an affair. I never imagined I would have to deal with something like this. Not with how close we've always been. Not to mention how much we've always loved each other."

"Celine, people grow apart every single day. It's unfortunate, but it happens. It's life."

Celine didn't bother responding, and Keith left and went upstairs. Celine followed behind him, and to her surprise, he went into the guest bedroom again. She knew he'd slept there the last two nights, but after hearing her news, she'd expected him to have at least a little more compassion. Regardless of how he was feeling about their marriage, she was still his wife and the mother of his child. But who was she fooling? His compassion for her was gone, because he was sleeping with someone else. He still wouldn't admit it, but he also *still* wouldn't deny it. His attitude was cocky, and he acted as though he didn't care whether they stayed married or not—this, of course, was usually the case when any man had found himself a plan B. Whenever a man allowed another woman to enter the picture, he became bold and heartless, and he didn't feel bad about it. This was true of all men who decided that being unhappy justified their having an affair. These same men stupidly believed they could live perfect lives with some graceless whore.

Celine loved her husband and she wanted to fight for her marriage, but she also wouldn't keep begging him to do right by her. She wouldn't be foolish. She wouldn't continue wasting time on a man—husband or not—who wanted to be somewhere else, especially when her real energies should be directed toward trying to stay alive. There was no telling how things were going to turn out after Tuesday, so she would spend this holiday weekend praying and meditating. She would focus on God and worry about Keith later. It was just the way things had to be—whether she liked it or not.

Chapter 10

eline, Kassie, and Lauren walked into the sanctuary of Deliverance Outreach, stepped inside one of the middle rows, and took their seats. They'd arrived just in time, as the eleven o'clock Sunday morning service was about to begin. Normally Celine was totally at peace when she came to church, but today she felt completely out of sorts. This was the reason she'd almost stayed in bed and not gotten up at all, but then Kassie had expressed how much she wanted them to go. Lauren had called to check on her as well and had suggested that church was a good place for her to be. Celine had agreed, but ever since confronting Keith yesterday morning, right after he'd moseyed in just before dawn, she'd been a little down. She'd stayed in bed, sleeping most of the day so she wouldn't have to fixate on her problems. Even when it had come time to pick up Kassie on Saturday evening from Delia's two-day birthday celebration, it had taken everything in Celine to throw on the first pieces of clothing she saw. Celine had never been a depressed kind of person, but for the last twenty-four hours, that was exactly the way she'd felt. And it wasn't getting any better. Maybe if she could make sense of all that was happening, things wouldn't be so bad, but truth was, she couldn't. She had no understanding of why she was enduring so much emotional pain, and she wondered what she'd done to deserve it. She was well aware that everyone reaped what they sowed, but this sure did seem like a lot.

Kassie looked around the sanctuary and then at her mom, smiling. She was such a good child who had an amazing sweet spirit, and she deserved to have her mother here for as long as possible. Celine knew it was selfish to think that way—particularly since she knew only God had the ability to decide how long anyone could be here—but the human side of her wanted to remain with her daughter for as long as possible. Celine wanted to celebrate each of Kassie's birthday milestones—her twelfth, sixteenth, eighteenth, twenty-first, twenty-fifth, thirtieth, fortieth, and fiftieth. She knew forty more years was a lot to ask for, but she couldn't help wanting every last bit of it. She also looked forward to seeing her daughter graduating high school and college and then getting married to a man who would love and cherish her until death. Celine certainly couldn't wait to have grandchildren one day.

She wanted all this and more, except her faith had diminished to an all-time low. There were days when she easily trusted and believed that everything would work out, but then there were days like today when she knew for sure that her marriage would end in divorce and that she had only a matter of months to live. She knew her thinking was irrational, what with her not having a final diagnosis, but for some reason she couldn't control her pessimism. Since discovering the lump in her breast, she'd been terrified and she couldn't get past it.

When the choir finished singing their first selection of the morning, one of Deliverance Outreach's male soloists walked over to the microphone. As soon as he sang the first line of "I Need You Now," water filled Celine's eyes. Then, when she heard the words "I need you right away," tears rolled down her face nonstop. Lauren passed her a handkerchief and placed her arm around her. Kassie reached and held her mom's hand. Celine cried because she truly did need God right now. She needed Him to fix things. Make her whole again.

When the soloist finished the song, Pastor Curtis Black walked up the steps and stood at the glass podium. "This is the day the Lord hath made, so let us rejoice and be glad in it."

"Amen," the congregation said.

"As always, it's good to be in the house of the Lord. It's great to have yet one more opportunity to worship and praise Him. It's an honor and a blessing to have Him in our lives."

*Amen*s rang throughout the sanctuary.

Pastor Black looked across the sanctuary. "It just

feels good to know Him. It feels good to know that our Lord and Savior Jesus Christ loved us so much that He was willing to die for us. He was willing to trust and believe His Father no matter what. Of course, we all know that when Jesus went into the Garden of Gethsemane to pray, temptation and fear tried to overtake Him, but in the end, He trusted God. Almost just as quickly as He asked His Father if there was some way that this cup could pass from Him, He prayed a second time, saying that if it wasn't possible, then let Thy will be done. This is the part that still sends chills through me every single time I read Matthew twenty-six. You see, Jesus knew that what He was about to go through was going to be hard and painful. But no matter what, He knew that obeying God's Word meant everything. He believed wholeheartedly in what His Father had promised Him — He believed that all would be well. And it was."

Celine sniffled and nodded in agreement.

"So today," Pastor Black said, "I want to speak on the topic Faith, Trust, and Belief."

Celine pulled out her tablet and opened her Bible app, waiting for Pastor Black to tell them which scriptures he'd be reading. Lauren did the same.

"If you'll turn with me to Psalms ninety-one, two," he said, allowing a few seconds for everyone to find it. "And it says, 'I will say of the Lord, He is my refuge and my fortress: my God; in him will I trust.' Then, if you'll turn to Psalms fifty-six, three and four. 'What time I am afraid, I will trust in thee. In God I will praise his word, in God, I have put my trust; I will not fear what flesh can do unto me.'"

Celine read this scripture again, even after Pastor Black had moved on to others. *What time I am afraid, I will trust in thee. In God I will praise his word, in God I have put my trust; I will not fear what flesh can do unto me.* Celine had seen and heard these two verses before, but it wasn't until now that she paid close attention to them. Here she'd been crying, complaining, and feeling down for days when her focus should have been more on God. It was always so easy for folks to claim they trusted and believed in Him—including her—but deep down, they looked for the worst to happen. They allowed fear and doubt to set in, and faith escaped them. Trust and belief became nonexistent. Celine had allowed the same thing to happen to her, but not anymore. And in seconds, she felt her spirit being renewed. God had spoken to her mind and heart, and she'd heard Him. So from this moment on, she was going to depend on God the way she'd been taught by her mom and her maternal grandparents. No matter how tough the road ahead might be, she wouldn't give in to it.

Pastor Black turned his Bible. "And finally, one of the simplest yet most meaningful scriptures of all is Proverbs three and five, which says, 'Trust in the Lord with all thine heart; and lean not to your own understanding.'"

Celine reread this scripture as well. *Trust in the Lord with all thine heart, and lean not to your own understanding.*

She closed her eyes, mentally reciting the words over and over. *Trust in the Lord with all thine heart, and lean not to your own understanding. Trust in the Lord with all thine heart, and lean not to your own understanding…*

Celine felt tears filling her eyes again, even while closed, but this time she cried with joy. Not because she knew what would happen with her biopsy, but because she felt God's presence and she believed He would handle everything. Cancer or not, she was going to be fine. With God's help she would deal with whatever was coming. With His love, she would prevail in the manner He chose.

Chapter 11

Celine waited for Dr. Jones and his nurse, Tina, to leave the procedure room, and then she got off the table and removed her surgical gown. They'd just completed the biopsy, and thank God they'd only given her local anesthesia, because she'd ended up having to go to the doctor's office alone. It wasn't like she hadn't been able to drive herself there or that she wouldn't be able to drive back home, it was the moral support she'd needed and wanted. It was her husband, who she'd asked to be there for her. But as she should have easily expected, Keith had told her he couldn't reschedule his morning meetings and that he was sorry. He'd even gone as far as saying, "Can't Lauren go with you?" but Celine hadn't bothered responding. She'd not said another word to him from that point on. Then, before he'd left for work, he'd rattled off an uncaring "Good luck with everything," which had sounded as though he were speaking to someone he barely knew. Celine had actually considered calling Lauren the way Keith had suggested, but she still wasn't ready to discuss the problems they were having. She certainly didn't want to talk about those issues today, not when it had taken every prayer she could muster, trying to prepare for her biopsy appointment. And now that it was over, she had to concentrate on meditating and praying until she received her results.

When Celine was fully dressed, Tina knocked on the door and walked back in, smiling. "How are you feeling?"

"Fine."

"The area where the needle was inserted is still numb, but even when the numbness fades, you shouldn't have much soreness. If you do have some discomfort, taking Tylenol or ibuprofen should help. Then, of course, if you find that you're having severe pain or you see swelling or redness, you should call us right away. And here's some postbiopsy information you can take with you," Tina said, passing a couple of documents to Celine.

Celine took them but didn't say anything.

"Do you have any questions?" Tina asked.

"No, not really."

"Well, if you do, just let us know."

"Thank you, and all I can hope is that we have the results sooner rather than later."

"I hope so, too. With your having your biopsy this morning, though, there really is a good chance we'll have your results by late tomorrow afternoon. At the latest, on Thursday."

Celine grabbed her handbag.

Tina opened the door to the examination room. "You take care, and please call us if you need to."

"I will, and thanks again."

Celine left Dr. Jones's office and went out to the parking lot. When she sat inside her car, she debated calling her brother. She'd been wanting to call him all along, but for whatever reason, she was still holding out and waiting to see what her final diagnosis was. So she decided to stick to the plan.

She pulled out the postprocedure paperwork and scanned it. She read down the list of dos and don'ts, and she was kind of bummed when she read that she was supposed to take it easy for the rest of the day. She didn't feel sick or tired, and since there was a great chance she'd be having surgery soon, she needed to get as much work done as possible. She had two marketing campaigns to complete, and although this was the final month for both of them, she always liked working and doing all she could for her clients until the very end. She went above and beyond, trying to give them the kind of service they'd paid for and then some.

But in addition to those two clients, Celine had also heard from a top advertising firm in Chicago that she'd been wanting to contract with for a long time. However, now she would have to wait until she heard from Dr. Jones. The last thing she wanted was to have to pass on working with them, but she might not have a choice.

It took Celine about twenty minutes to get home, and now she was turning into her driveway. She pressed the garage door opener, but instead of driving inside, she did something she hadn't done in months. She sat admiring the exterior of their beautifully land-scaped tan brick home. Mostly she thought about the day she and Keith had first looked at it and how thrilled they'd been. Kassie had only been four years old, but even she'd been excited when she'd seen it. Celine and Keith had found their dream home, and they couldn't have been happier. But that was then; six years ago, when every aspect of their lives had been full of bliss. Celine hadn't been able to imagine a life better than the one she had with Keith and Kassie. She hadn't counted on all that was happening now with her marriage.

Celine went inside the house, and while she knew she wasn't supposed to be working, she grabbed a bottle of water from the refrigerator and headed down the hallway to her office. She sat down and scrolled through her email. She opened and answered only those messages that were important, and eventually she reviewed her to-do list.

But then she thought she heard someone coming inside the house, which didn't make sense because it wasn't quite noon yet. She also rarely forgot to set the alarm system, even in the middle of the day, but she had this time. She was sure she'd locked the door leading from the kitchen to the garage, though.

"Keith?" she yelled out, hoping it was him.

"Yeah, it's me," he said.

Celine scrunched her forehead, wondering why he was home so early.

Keith stood in front of her doorway for a moment but then walked in and sat on the small sofa.

"What's wrong?" she asked.

"How did your appointment go?"

"Well, if you'd gone with me, I'm sure it could've been better."

"Celine, please. I mean, it wasn't like they were putting you under. You were more than able to drive to and from there with no problem."

"That's beside the point, Keith. I still needed you to be there."

"Look," he said, "I don't want to argue. The reason I came home was so we could talk."

"About what?"

"Us, and the fact that I just can't do this anymore."

"Do what?"

"Live here. Stay in an unhappy marriage."

Celine stared at him like he was an alien. There was no way she'd heard him correctly.

"So you don't have anything to say?" he asked.

"Please tell me you're not serious."

"I'm very serious. I'm sorry, but we can't go on like this."

Celine relaxed further in her chair, folding her arms and shaking her head. "I don't believe you. You're actually going to leave me for some skank you're sleeping with? You're going to leave your daughter because of some whore?"

"I told you before," he said. "I've been unhappy for more than a year, and you never even noticed. You were too busy working and doing whatever else you wanted."

"But I didn't know. And while you may have complained a couple of times, it wasn't like you ever sat me down for a real conversation. You never told me how you really felt. You just went out and found someone."

"We've gone over all this before. It's not about someone else. It's about you and me. I wish things were different, but this is what it's come to."

"No, this is what you've *decided* for both of us."

"My feelings aren't the same, and I can't keep pretending."

"Really?" she said, raising her eyebrows. "So are you saying you don't love me?"

"I don't know."

"How could you not know?"

"I just don't. I mean, I guess a part of me will always love you because we have a child together, but it's not the same."

"Do you love her?"

Keith gazed at her, not saying anything.

"Do you?"

Keith paused and then said, "I don't know."

Celine didn't know which felt worse: the knife he'd used to stab her in the back or the dagger he was pounding straight through her heart. It just didn't seem real. And how could it, when she honestly hadn't seen this coming? Was this the new norm? Husbands going months and months being unhappy and not communicating their true feelings to their wives? Did sex with some trick automatically trump twelve years of marriage? Could a man actually stop loving his wife and then start loving some desperate tramp who couldn't find her own man? Celine would never have believed it before now, but clearly the answer was yes.

"So you're in love with someone else? How long have you been seeing her, Keith?"

"I really don't want to talk about that. It's not going to help or change anything."

"What about my test results? What if I have cancer?"

Keith scooted to the edge of the sofa. "I'm sorry about the timing, but I just can't put my life on hold any longer. I'm moving out by the end of the week."

"Do you even hear what you're saying? You're going to leave your own wife to fend for herself? What about in sickness and in health, Keith? Have you forgotten about that?"

"Like I said, I'm sorry."

"Sorry isn't going to cut it!" she shouted.

Keith got to his feet and turned to walk out of Celine's office. "I'm sorry, but my mind is made up."

"I hate you," she said, picking up her stapler and throwing it at him as hard as she could.

It struck the center of his back. "Ouch! Are you crazy?"

"No, you're the one who's gone insane."

Keith shook his head at her and walked away.

Celine rushed behind him, shoving him.

He turned toward her. "You'd better stop while you're ahead."

"And if I don't?"

"Just keep it up, and you'll see."

"Are you threatening me?" she said, moving closer to him.

"I'm giving you fair warning. I know you're hurt, and you just came from the doctor, but if you put your hands on me again..."

"You're not going to do a thing to me, Keith. And if you do, you'll regret it from now on."

"Whatever," he said, and went upstairs.

Celine didn't know whether to cry, curse, or scream. She was full of emotions, and she couldn't think straight. On the one hand, she wanted to hurt Keith physically, and on the other, she wanted to beg him not to leave her. She felt like a complete fool. Keith and his whore had messed around for a while, and the joke was on Celine—except Celine wasn't laughing. She felt like committing murder, and the only thing that stopped her was Kassie. It wasn't fair for Kassie to lose both her mother and father—one to prison and one to death—so Celine took a few deep breaths and calmed herself down. She was still hurt, but she had to pull herself together before her daughter got home. She had to be strong, even when she wasn't.

Chapter 12

The phone rang, and Celine's heart skipped a beat. It was just after two p.m. on Wednesday, and while she'd been waiting nervously for this very call, she paused before answering. The caller ID screen showed that it was Dr. Jones's office, but she debated letting it go to voice mail. In a split second, she grabbed the phone from its base and answered it.

"Hello?"

"Celine?" Dr. Jones said.

"Yes," she answered, knowing that the only time a doctor called a patient directly was when the news was serious. Still, she held her breath.

"I have your pathology report back, and I'm afraid your tumor is cancerous."

Celine breathed freely now, but her nerves were shot. On Sunday, she'd decided that she wouldn't worry and that she was prepared for whatever the outcome of her biopsy would be, but this morning, she'd become upset again.

"So where do we go from here?" she asked.

"I'd definitely like to schedule a lumpectomy as soon as possible, and the good news is that you're only at stage two, and I don't believe you'll need chemo. I won't know that for sure until I remove your tumor and send it over to pathology, but if I'm right, then you'll only need radiation. That would be five days per week for six weeks, though."

Celine felt like she was having an out-of-body experience.

"So you think you'll be able to get it all?"

"I think we're in a great position. There's no way I can guarantee anything, but if we can remove all the cells through surgery and radiation, that will be a huge plus."

"Well, I trust your judgment, and I trust God, so I'm good."

"I'm glad you feel that way, and let me just say that your overall attitude will make a world of difference. Being positive about every aspect of this will help you tremendously."

"I'll remember that."

"Sounds good. Tina will call you to get you scheduled, but if you have any questions, please don't hesitate to call."

"Thank you so much, Doctor. I will, and I really appreciate it."

"No problem, and you hang in there."

"Thank you again."

Celine hung up the phone and sat for a few minutes. *Dear Lord, help me to be strong for my daughter. Give me what I need to get through this. Lord, I trust You, I believe in You, I have faith in You.*

Celine sighed and felt somewhat better, so she picked up her phone to call Lauren. Normally Keith would have been the first person she contacted with any important news, but right now, she needed to talk to someone who genuinely cared about her. Thankfully, Lauren answered on the second ring.

"This is Lauren speaking."

"Hey," Celine said.

"Hey, how are you? Have you heard from the doctor yet?"

"He just called, and the tumor is cancerous."

"I'll be there as soon as I can."

"You really don't have to leave work. I'm okay."

"I'll see you in about an hour. Maybe less than that."

"Thanks, girl."

"I love you much."

"I love you, too."

Celine set the phone down and thought about Kassie. Her class had ventured over to Chicago on an end-of-the-school-year field trip, and Celine was sort of glad she wouldn't be back until around six. That way she could talk to Lauren for a couple of hours and mentally prepare how she was going to explain things to Kassie. Celine dreaded the conversation already, but it had to be done.

Celine thought about things for a few minutes and then made the call she'd been putting off for days. Jackson answered as soon as she finished dialing.

"Hey, Sis, what's up? I've been meaning to call you for the last couple of days. We haven't talked in over a week, and you know that's not like us. I've really been busy at work, though. A lot busier than usual. But how are you?"

He sounded so upbeat that Celine hated having to tell him why she was calling.

"Not too good, and there's something I need to tell you."

"What's that?"

"I have breast cancer."

"You have what?"

"Breast cancer. My doctor did a biopsy, and he just called me with the results."

"Biopsy? When did you find out you needed one?"

"I found a lump a little over a week ago."

"And you're just telling me about it? Why?"

"I didn't want to worry you, and I was hoping there wouldn't be anything to tell."

"You're wrong for that, Sis. How could you keep something like that from me? Your own brother? We're all we've got."

"I know, Jack," she said, "and I'm sorry."

"So now what? Are you having surgery?"

"Yes."

"When?"

"Soon. They'll be calling me with a date."

"Well, I hope you'll at least let me know that right away."

"Of course I will. I'll call you as soon as I know."

"So are you having a mastectomy?"

"No, he thinks removing the tumor will be enough, but I'll also need to have six weeks of radiation. Thirty treatments in all."

"That's all fine and well, but why don't you just have your whole breast removed? That way you have a better chance of it not coming back."

"Dr. Jones says I'm only at stage two, so he thinks I'll be fine. And what do you know about mastectomies, anyway?"

"One of my coworkers' wife was diagnosed with breast cancer."

"What stage was she in?"

"Third."

"Well, Dr. Jones is one of the best in the area, so I have to trust his opinion on this."

"You have to do what you feel is right, but I just thought I'd ask."

"I appreciate it, and you know I love you."

"I love you, too, and as soon as you know more, I'll be making my airline reservations."

"You don't have to do that. The procedure will be outpatient, so I'll be home by afternoon or evening."

"Having any surgery is still a risk. So I'm coming, and that's all there is to it."

Celine smiled because even though she didn't want to burden him, she needed her brother there with her.

"And hey," he said, "how are Keith and Kassie doing? How are they taking the news?"

Celine had been hoping Jackson wouldn't ask about

his brother-in-law, but now that he had, she wasn't going to hide anything else from him.

"He's leaving me."

"What do you mean?"

"He's moving out."

"Why?"

"Says he's unhappy, and he doesn't want to be here anymore."

"And he knows you have breast cancer?"

"No, but I told him a few days ago that the doctor was pretty sure I did."

"And what did he say?"

"Not a lot, and yesterday all he did was apologize for the timing."

"That bastard! He's going to leave you while you're sick? Who does that? I oughta jump on a plane and come tear that clown apart."

"Jack, please."

"Please, what? Did that fool even go with you to your appointments?"

"Jack, listen to me," she said. "I'm fine. Really."

"Did he or didn't he?"

"No, but what does that matter now?"

"It matters a lot, and the only way a man acts like this is when he's laying up with some skank. Period."

"I can't worry about that," she said. "I have to worry about Kassie and my surgery."

Jackson sighed loudly. "You're right. I'm sorry if I upset you, but I don't like what Keith is doing to you. I don't like it at all."

"I know, but you can't make someone be with you if they don't want to. Am I hurt? Of course I am. Do I wish he'd change his mind? Absolutely. Will staying mad and losing sleep change anything? Definitely not. So I've got to focus on me right now."

"I agree. I'm just stunned. I had no idea things were bad between you and Keith."

"Neither did I. At least not this bad, anyway."

"I'm so sorry you're having to deal with all of this, and like I said, please let me know as soon as you find out your surgery date. That way, I can let my manager know I need some time off."

Jackson was a senior systems analyst for a pharmaceutical company, and Celine was proud of all that her brother had accomplished. Especially since it had taken him eight years of being an undergrad to find himself. He'd always been a straight-A student, but changing his major three different times had extended his graduation date. Now, though, he had not only a bachelor's but a master's, too. Jackson was just a year younger than Celine, but she still saw him as her baby brother—and whether he liked it or not, that would never change. Although now the tables would need to turn a little. Because of her illness, she was counting on him to be her protector. She no longer had her parents to turn to, but she knew Jackson would be there for her in every way possible. He and Lauren would never let her down. Not even if their lives depended on it.

* * *

Lauren had arrived about a half hour ago, and Celine had told her that Keith was moving out.

"Surely you must be making this up," she said.

"I wish I were, but I'm not. He's having an affair, and he wants out."

"How long has this been going on?"

"I don't know. He just started staying out late, and two Sundays ago was the first time he was gone past midnight. He didn't come home until five a.m."

"Wow."

"I was just as shocked as you are. Keith has never done anything like this before."

"And he just started this for no reason? You didn't notice anything was wrong?"

"Not really. He says I haven't been paying him any attention."

"Please. That's just an excuse. I mean, work and everything else can sometimes get in the way of any relationship, but he couldn't come to you like a man? He couldn't express what he was feeling?"

"Those are my thoughts exactly."

"So he just went out and found some tramp?"

"I guess so. At first he wouldn't admit it, but he also never denied it. Then, yesterday, I asked him if he loved her, and he said he didn't know."

"This is crazy, and it just goes to show that you can't trust anyone."

"Tell me about it. But if he wants out, he wants out."

"I just think it's pretty awful, though, that Keith is leaving right before you have surgery. It just doesn't get more low-down than that, and I'm really disappointed in him. And what about Kassie?"

"I know, I've already told him all that, but he doesn't seem to care. All he's thinking about is being with his woman," Celine said, starting to feel sad again, and Lauren must have noticed.

"I am so, so sorry. Here I came over to support you, yet I'm obsessing over Keith and what he's doing to you."

"It's not a problem. I know this is taking you totally by surprise, and you're upset. I'm upset, too, but I can't spend all my time worrying about Keith. What I have to do now is try to stay as calm as I can. I need to meditate and pray more than ever before and be here for Kassie."

"You're right, and I'm going to be here for both of you."

"I appreciate that, and Jackson says he'll be home for my surgery, too."

"Good. I'm glad you called him."

"The one thing I am going to have to figure out, though, is how I'll get to all my radiation treatments. Because Dr. Jones is already planning for that to happen. I might be able to drive myself to the first few, but I saw online that one of the common symptoms of radiation is heavy fatigue. Everyone is different, but I still need to prepare for it."

"We'll get all that worked out when the time comes.

So please don't worry about that. I'm also going to plan on taking a week of vacation when you have your surgery. That way, when you come home, I can stay here with you. Someone is going to need to cook, wash, and clean."

Celine listened as Lauren sat figuring out everything, and she thanked God for her best friend. She was grateful to have Lauren in her life, since she no longer had a husband to depend on; at least not one who cared what happened to her. He was only concerned about himself, and that made Celine think about something else. Not only would she have to sit Kassie down this evening to explain about her cancer and surgery, she and Keith would also need to tell her he was leaving. Celine was having a hard time digesting both pieces of news herself, so she couldn't imagine how traumatized Kassie would be. Her heart would be broken like never before, and the thought of it all made Celine's own heart ache. Too much was happening way too fast, and Celine just hoped Kassie could survive it. She prayed that God would protect her daughter completely.

Chapter 13

Celine walked upstairs and then down the hall to Kassie's room. Kassie had her door slightly closed, and Celine could hear her singing along with one of her favorite Disney Channel characters. She sounded so happy, and it killed Celine to have to tell her about her illness. It wasn't the kind of thing you wanted to tell any child, and Celine prayed for strength.

She knocked on her daughter's door.

"Come in," Kassie said in her same singing voice.

Celine opened the door. "Hey, sweetie, can you pause that for a minute?"

"Okay," she said. She was sitting in bed on top of her comforter, resting against three pillow shams.

Celine sat on the side of the bed, facing her.

"What's wrong, Mom? You look sad again. You look sad a lot."

"I know, honey, but I don't mean to."

"Are you okay? I'm starting to get scared."

"Well, that's what I wanted to talk to you about. Mom's going to need surgery."

"Why?"

"I have a lump in my breast."

Kassie looked at her mom's chest. "Which one?"

"My left one."

"So your doctor is going to take it out?"

"Yes."

"Does it hurt?"

"No."

"Then why do you have to have surgery?"

"Because it wouldn't be good to let it stay in there. My doctor wants to remove it before it gets bigger."

"If it does, will it make you sick?"

"Yes."

Kassie stared at her mom, seemingly trying to decide whether she should say what she was thinking.

"What is it, honey?" Celine asked.

"Do you have cancer?"

Celine had sort of been hoping she wouldn't have to use that word, but she also wasn't going to lie to her daughter.

"I do, but how do you know about cancer?"

"Delia's aunt had it. Remember?"

"I'd forgotten about that, but yes, she did."

"Are you going to die like her?"

Celine grabbed both of Kassie's hands. "No, sweetie. They caught mine very early. Once I heal up from my surgery, though, I'll need to have something called radiation."

"Will that hurt?"

"No, but I might be a little tired from it."

"Will you have to stay in the hospital a long time?"

"No. When I have my surgery, I'll be home later that same day. I won't have to stay there for any of my radiation treatments, either."

"Will I be able to come to the hospital with you?"

"Not for the surgery, but you'll see me after school."

"Is Daddy going to be off work so he can take care of you?"

Celine tried to think quickly, but she wasn't sure how to answer. The same as she hadn't wanted to lie about her diagnosis, she didn't want to lie about Keith.

"I'm going to have a lot of people helping to take care of me."

"Like Auntie Lauren and Uncle Jackson?"

"Yes, and they'll be helping take care of you as well."

"I'm glad, because I don't think Daddy can take care of us by himself. Remember that time you had the flu, Mom?" she said, giggling. "He burned up our breakfast, and then he burned the shirt he was trying to iron. And then he accidentally put some bleach on our jeans!" she said, laughing louder.

Celine couldn't help laughing with her. "Yeah, I remember all right."

"That was funny," she said, still smiling.

"But back to what we were talking about. Do you have any questions?"

"Can I catch your cancer? I mean, when I get older, will I have it, too?"

Celine hadn't been counting on this particular question, either. Not from a ten-year-old. But then,

Kassie had always been wise beyond her years. She had both book and common sense.

"Well, it's not contagious, but none of us ever knows what we might get down the road. Our job is to pray that God protects us and keeps us healthy."

"Is that why you got sick? Because we didn't pray enough? I pray for me, you, Daddy, Uncle Jackson, Auntie Lauren, and all my friends every night. But maybe I didn't say the right things."

"Oh, sweetie," Celine said, caressing her daughter's face. "This isn't your fault. It's nobody's fault, okay?"

Kassie didn't seem convinced, but she didn't argue.

"You hear me?" Celine said. "There's nothing you could have done to prevent this from happening."

"You really mean that?"

"Yes."

"Well, then why did this happen to you?"

"Because it just did. People sometimes get sick, but then they get better."

"I hope you get better really soon. I don't want you to be sick."

"I don't want to be sick, either, and I believe God is going to heal me."

"I believe He will, too. Pastor Black says that we just have to ask and believe about anything, and that's what I'm going to do, Mom."

"Good for you. And no matter what, I want you to know that I love you and I always will."

Kassie moved closer to the edge of the bed next to her mom and hugged her. "I love you, too, Mom, and

I'll do anything you want. I'll help you the whole time until you get better."

Celine held her baby girl tightly, trying to fight back tears. Kassie was so innocent and caring. So loving and genuine. She was a major blessing from God and the kind of daughter every parent should have.

After watching the rest of Kassie's Disney program with her, Celine went downstairs to her office. But then she heard Keith walking in. She knew he might try avoiding her, so she went into the kitchen.

"We need to talk," she said.

"I already told you my mind is made up."

"That's not what this is about, and since I don't want Kassie to hear us, I need to talk to you privately."

Celine could tell from Keith's body language that she was the last person he wanted to be closed up in a room with. But he followed her back to her office anyway.

Celine shut the door. "Didn't my biopsy results cross your mind at all today?"

"No, because I wasn't even sure when you'd have them."

"Well, Dr. Jones called this afternoon, and my tumor is malignant."

"I'm sorry to hear that, but I know you'll be fine."

"Yes, I will be," she said matter-of-factly, and Keith looked shocked.

"You sound a lot more confident than you did a couple of days ago, and I'm glad to see it."

Celine shook her head. "You never cease to amaze

me, you know that? But right now you're the least of my worries. Kassie is my main concern, and she should also be yours."

"What is that supposed to mean? I love my daughter, and I'm always going to be there for her."

"How?"

"What do you mean, how?"

"How can you move out and still be here for her?"

"Easily."

"Yeah, well, we'll see."

"I guess we will."

For a second and only a second, Celine had wanted to plead with him to postpone his plans, at least until she finished her radiation treatments. But no matter how much she still loved him, she wouldn't beg a man who'd become as cruel as Hitler. She wouldn't ask him to do anything, not when he was callous enough to leave a daughter who adored him.

"So when do you want to tell Kassie that we're separating?" he said.

Celine frowned. "Separating? No, you've got it all wrong. What you're doing is walking out on us."

Keith glared at her. "Why do you insist on trying to make things difficult?"

"This is all your doing, but just so you know, we're not telling Kassie anything tonight."

"And why not?"

"Because I just told her about my surgery. She had a lot of questions about cancer, and we're not piling any more bad news on her."

"Fine, but it'll have to be tomorrow or Friday because I'm moving out on Saturday."

Celine wanted to ask him why he was moving in such a hurry, but she still didn't have the energy to do it.

"I'm really sorry you're sick," he said, opening the door. "I'm sorry about everything."

"Please don't say that anymore."

"What?"

"How sorry you are. If you were *that* sorry, we wouldn't be having this conversation. You never would have started sleeping around, and you wouldn't be abandoning your daughter. You wouldn't be deserting either one of us."

"I can't talk to you when you're like this," he said, and left.

Celine knew it wasn't right to hate anyone, but she was starting to feel that way about Keith. She was beginning to loathe the ground he walked on, and she knew that wasn't good. She was hurt, but she was also infuriated. She was trying her best not to become a woman scorned, however, Keith wasn't making it easy. He was pushing her to her limit, and she wanted to get back at him. Maybe then she could feel better about all this. Although, truth was, she didn't have to do anything. The reason: Everyone on this earth paid a price for treating people badly, and Keith would be no different.

Chapter 14

This was a call Celine had hoped she wouldn't have to make. But she also knew it wasn't fair to keep them waiting and wondering when she knew she couldn't work with them.

She dialed the prestigious advertising firm in Chicago that had contacted her earlier this week.

"Tom Blakely's office," the woman said.

"Hi. My name is Celine Richardson. Tom contacted me about a marketing campaign, and I was wondering if he was in."

"Yes, of course. I know he's been waiting to hear back from you. I'll send you right through."

"Thank you."

After a couple of seconds, Tom came on the line.

"Celine? How are you?"

"To tell you the truth, not as well as I'd like to be. I just learned yesterday that I'll need to have surgery."

"Oh no. I'm very sorry to hear that, and I hope it's not too serious."

Celine wasn't planning to tell anyone in the industry

about her illness. Maybe once she'd been given a clean bill of health, but not before then. "I'll be down for a little while, but I'm sure I'll be fine. Unfortunately, though, I'm going to have to pass on your offer."

"I assumed as much, but I hope you'll let me know when you're available again. We really would love to work with you."

"I appreciate hearing that, and I will definitely be in touch."

"You take good care of yourself, and I wish you well with everything."

"Thanks, Tom."

"You're quite welcome."

Celine prepared to set her phone on her desk, but it rang. It was Dr. Jones's office.

"Hello?" she said.

"Celine?"

"Yes?"

"Hi, this is Tina."

"Hi, how are you?"

"I'm good, and I hope you are, too. I'm calling because we've scheduled your lumpectomy for next Friday at Mitchell Memorial."

"Okay."

"That's a week from tomorrow, so the pre-op department will be calling you soon. Maybe even this afternoon or evening. They'll be asking you questions about your medical history and then explaining what you'll need to do to prepare for surgery. They'll also be getting preapproval from your insurance company. The other thing they'll probably ask is whether you have a living will and/or a health care power-of-attorney document in place."

"Sounds good."

"Do you have any questions I can answer for you?"

"No, I don't think so."

"Okay, then, Dr. Jones will see you next week."

"Thank you for calling."

"Anytime, and bye for now."

"Good-bye."

Celine had hoped her surgery would be scheduled as soon as possible, but now that it had, a bit of fear had set in again. Ever since waking up a few hours ago, she'd been keeping her faith strong, however, she suddenly felt weak and as though things weren't going to turn out very well. She knew Dr. Jones had stated her cancer was at stage two, but what if once he removed the tumor, he learned something different? What if her cancer had spread to her lymph nodes or to some other area of her body? What if having a mastectomy was a better option? Should she maybe ask Dr. Jones about it? Or maybe a better question was, did she even *want* to have one? What if Dr. Jones removed the tumor, and he didn't get it all? What if she ended up having to have yet another surgery, and maybe even chemo? What if she didn't survive at all?

Celine reflected on one question after another and then realized how useless it was. Worrying and trying to figure out what might happen wasn't doing her any good. It was upsetting her unnecessarily, and she had to move on to something else. So she called Lauren.

"Hey, how are you?" Lauren said.

"Okay, I guess. Did I catch you at a bad time?"

"No, not at all. But what's wrong? Because you definitely don't sound okay."

"Dr. Jones's nurse called, and my surgery is next Friday. But after I hung up with her, my mind spun in every direction. I thought about everything imaginable."

"I'm sure, but you've got to think only positive thoughts. You have to trust God and mean it, girl. You can't put your faith in Him today and then lose it the very next. You have to ask, believe, and wait for Him to deliver. You have to believe He'll do exactly what He says He'll do."

"You're right. I know you are, and I've got to do better than I have been. I have to release everything to Him and leave it there."

"You really do, and in time you will."

"I think it's the unknown that bothers me. I've never dealt with something like this before, and cancer is no joke. It's nothing to take lightly."

"That's true, but Dr. Jones has already given you a great prognosis. Surgery, radiation, and no chemo, right?"

"Yep, unless he discovers something more when he removes the tumor."

"He won't. He'll get everything while he's in there, and your pathology report will come back clean."

"I agree, and actually, if you want to know the truth, I'm more worried about Kassie than I am about myself. This won't be easy for her."

"No, but we'll get through it. And by the way, is Keith talking any differently?"

"No, he's moving out two days from now."

"I just can't believe he's really doing this, and I'm really starting to dislike him," Lauren said. "Keith used to be one of my favorite people, but not anymore."

"I feel the same way, but there's nothing I can do about it."

"Well, what I do know is this: People like Keith always get what is coming to them. Sometimes tenfold."

"Exactly," Celine said, wondering how all this would play out. But more than anything she wondered *when* it would.

Chapter 15

"No, Daddy! Why?" Kassie said, jumping up from the sofa in the family room. She and Celine were sitting side by side, and Keith sat adjacent to them on the loveseat.

"Sweetheart, please try to calm down," Celine said.

"Why are you leaving us? Did I do something wrong?"

"No, sweetheart," he said. "You didn't do anything. This isn't your fault."

"Well, then why did you and Mom stop loving each other? Why are you moving out?"

Keith bit his lip, seemingly trying to figure out what to say, and Celine wanted to wring his neck. How dare he do this to their daughter?

"Honey," he said, "it's complicated. But please know that it won't change how much I love you. Your mom and I will always love you, no matter what."

"But why, Daddy?" she said, standing directly in front of him.

Keith grabbed one of her hands. "Sometimes adults

go through things they don't want to. It's very hard to explain, and I'm very sorry this is happening."

"But why can't you and Mom fix things and make them okay again?"

"I wish we could."

"Then why won't you?"

"It's just not that simple."

"Where are you moving to?" Kassie asked.

Celine wanted to know the same thing.

"Into a condo," he said.

"All by yourself?"

"Yep, and once I get situated you'll have your own bedroom."

"But I already have a bedroom."

"I know, honey, but you'll have one at my place, too."

Kassie fell into her dad's arms and burst into tears. "Daddy, please don't leave."

Keith held Kassie with tear-filled eyes, gazing at Celine. Celine didn't have an ounce of sympathy for him.

"I know this is hard," he told Kassie. "But we'll still be able to see each other and do things just like always."

"No, we won't," she said, still hugging him. "Not like now."

Keith didn't say anything else.

Kassie pulled away from him. "What about Mom's surgery? Who's going to help take care of her?"

"I'll try my best to be there."

Liar! was all Celine could think. Keith knew full well he wasn't going to be at the hospital or anywhere near during her recovery period.

"Mom," Kassie said, "please tell Daddy not to leave."

"I'm sorry, honey, but this is your dad's decision."

"Daddy, why do you wanna leave? Are you mad at me and Mom?"

"No, I'm not mad at you at all."

"But you are with Mom?"

"Look, sweetheart, I know this makes you sad, but for now, this is the way things are going to have to be."

Kassie wept again and rushed upstairs to her room.

Celine squinted her eyes. "You're pathetic."

"I'm doing what I have to do."

"No, you're doing what you *want* to do. You don't care about me or Kassie."

"I'll always love my daughter."

"You sure have a strange way of showing it."

"Kassie knows I love her, and eventually she'll understand my decision."

"You really believe that? Or are you only saying that so you won't have to feel bad about it?"

"I do believe it. Children are very resilient, and as long as I still spend time with Kassie, she'll be fine."

"What about child support?"

"What about it? You think I'm not going to take care of my own child?"

"I don't know anything. So we're going to have to come to some sort of an agreement."

"You're already worrying about money, I see."

"I'm not worried at all, but I suggest you do the right thing."

"Or what?"

"We'll let a judge handle it."

"You're a real piece of work," he said.

"No, I'm your wife. I'm also getting ready to have surgery and won't be able to work for a while. And this mortgage still needs to be paid."

"Please. You act like you're having brain surgery or something. Like you're going to be totally incapacitated and won't be able to do anything for months."

"Are you trying to say breast cancer isn't serious?"

"No, but I'm tired of you trying to play the victim," he said, standing up. "People get sick all the time, and they recover with no problem. They also don't hold pity parties the way you seem to be doing."

"Victim?" she said. "I have cancer, and you have the audacity to call me that? That's really low, Keith, but you know what? Every dog has his day."

"And?"

"We all get what we deserve."

Keith turned and headed toward the stairway. "I'm done with this conversation."

Celine didn't bother acknowledging his last comment, but she couldn't deny how hurt she was. She would never let him see it, but reality had finally settled in: She was married to a man she no longer knew, and he was leaving her. It was as if he'd up and decided one night, out of the blue, that he didn't love her and wanted out. But it was the same as she'd been thinking before: This wasn't just about their marriage or the breakdown of it. This was about a third party. A woman who was low enough to sleep with a married man. A tramp who had no problem doing all she could to try to convince someone else's husband to abandon his family. A whore who had figured out a way to fool Keith into believing she could be a better woman to him than his own wife was. Keith was just as much at fault—actually he was more at fault than this mistress of his, because he was the one who was married—but Celine despised any woman who was ruthless and cold-blooded enough to sleep with another woman's husband. It spoke volumes about a woman's character. Keith couldn't see it now, but a woman like that was capable of doing just about anything, and could never be trusted. As the old cliché went, the grass always looked greener on the other side. The only thing, though, was that it almost never was. This was a fact, and Keith would eventually realize it. He would learn this truth the same as other men had been discovering for decades.

Chapter 16

As Celine awakened from the anesthesia, she batted her eyes and squinted when the light hit them. She heard a few people talking, some in near whispers, and she realized she was in recovery. It seemed that no time had passed at all from when the surgical staff had wheeled her down to the operating room, yet her procedure was already over. She smiled when she thought about the way Lauren had stood by her this past week and how she'd prayed for Celine daily. Celine was also elated that her brother hadn't listened to her and had flown in yesterday as planned. But in a matter of seconds, Celine's happiness diminished. She wasn't sure why Keith's words had suddenly entered her mind, but she heard them repeatedly. *"I'm tired of you trying to play the victim...People get sick all the time...They also don't hold pity parties the way you seem to be doing."* Celine tried to forget about him and the cruel things he'd said, but soon tears rolled down either side of her face. Before long, she cried so uncontrollably that her chest and stomach heaved up and down.

"Celine, I'm Tessa," the fiftysomething nurse said. "Are you okay? Are you having a lot of pain?"

Celine shook her head no, but kept crying.

"Are you sure? Because if you're hurting, we can get you something to help with that."

Celine was still weeping too hard to answer verbally, so she shook her head again.

"Well, then what's wrong?" Tessa asked, rubbing Celine's arm.

Celine sniffled a few times and took deep breaths.

"I'm sorry you're so upset," Tessa said, pulling Kleenex from the table next to Celine's bed and passing it to her.

Celine gently wiped her face and sniffled. She sighed heavily.

Tessa smiled. "You're sure you're not hurting."

"No," Celine said, between deep breaths. "I'm... okay...I'm...fine."

"Would you like some ice water?"

Celine nodded yes.

Tessa lifted a plastic pitcher and poured some in a large cup that contained a straw.

Celine drank as much as she could and then laid her head back down.

"Your family is outside waiting, and you'll be able to see them soon."

"Thank you," she said, wiping her face and eyes again.

"Here's your call button." Tessa showed her.

Celine still felt a bit groggy, so she doubted she'd be

able to watch anything on television. Maybe she would turn it on, though, just to keep her mind occupied with something other than her separation from Keith.

Tessa left, and Celine lay there, flipping through the channels. She stopped when she saw an old episode of *Law & Order*. She loved this show, but she was also fighting to stay awake.

However, just as she was about to fall off to sleep again, there was a knock on her door.

"Hey, Sis," Jackson said, and Celine smiled. Her baby brother had always been exceptionally handsome, and though he'd be turning forty this fall, he hadn't aged much.

"Hey yourself," Celine said.

"Hey, girl," Lauren said.

"Hey."

Lauren smiled and held Celine's hand. "Didn't I tell you God was going to handle this? Dr. Jones says that your surgery went very well, and that he believes he got everything."

"That's really great to hear," Celine said. "God is so good."

"He absolutely is," Lauren agreed.

"I prayed more this last week than I have in years," Jackson added.

"Prayer means everything," Lauren said. "Both when things are bad and even when they're good."

There was another knock at the door, then Dr. Jones walked in.

"So how are you feeling?" he asked Celine.

"Pretty good. No pain."

"Good. Well, as I told your brother and friend, the surgery went as well as I expected. Your tumor was pretty isolated, but I do still want you to have six weeks of radiation just to make sure we didn't miss anything. We're also sending your tumor and sample lymph nodes on to pathology to be tested."

"Will we hear back soon?" Celine asked.

"Probably in two to three days. Not too long at all."

"And I still get to go home today?"

"Yes, that'll be fine. I want you to stay here in recovery until you're completely stable, but after that we'll be able to discharge you."

"Thank you for everything."

"You're quite welcome," he said, patting her leg through the bedspread. Then he shook Jackson's and Lauren's hands. "It was great meeting you both, and you two take good care of my patient here."

"We will, Doctor," Jackson told him. "We won't let her do anything she's not supposed to, which will be very interesting, but we're going to make her do the right thing."

Dr. Jones laughed and so did Lauren and Jackson, but Celine playfully rolled her eyes at her brother.

"She's used to being the boss of me," Jackson said, "so now it's my turn."

They all chuckled again.

"Have a good afternoon," Dr. Jones said.

Celine looked at Jackson. "I see you've got big-time jokes today, huh?"

"Yep. It's going to be good keeping tabs on you. Making you stay in bed and take it easy."

"Whatever. I'm still the oldest, though, and don't you forget it."

Lauren laughed at both of them.

"But seriously," Celine said, "I love you so much, baby brother, and I don't know what I would have done today if you and Lauren hadn't been here for me." Then Celine gazed at her best friend. "Thank you, girl. Thank you for being here for me at every end."

"I wouldn't have it any other way. What are friends for? Especially best friends?"

"Well, I really appreciate everything you've done, because these last few days have been some of the toughest of my life."

"I know," Lauren said, "but better days are ahead."

Jackson nodded. "Exactly. All of this is just temporary."

"It took me a while, but by yesterday I fully trusted and believed God was going to heal me. My faith is very strong right now, and I'm grateful for that."

"That's wonderful to hear," Lauren said.

Celine blinked her eyes, trying to keep them open.

"Why don't you get some rest," Lauren said.

Jackson sat down in the seat on the right side of Celine's bed. "Yeah, I think that's a good idea."

Lauren sat to the left of her. "We'll be right here when you wake up."

"I love you both," Celine said. "Oh, and Lauren, with Jackson staying through the weekend, you really don't have to spend the night. We'll be fine."

"Well, actually, sis, I'd rather she did. You know, just in case your bandage needs to be changed. Or something female-related goes wrong."

Celine and Lauren shook their heads at him.

"What? I'm serious. I'll do anything else, but I'll leave that sort of thing to Lauren."

Celine laughed but fought to keep her eyes open. Before long, she lost the battle and gave in.

Chapter 17

*I*t was ten a.m., and while Celine had forced a smile on her face for the last half hour, she couldn't do it anymore. Kassie had come in and sat with her for about twenty minutes, and Jackson and Lauren had looked in on her, but now she was glad they'd all gone to other areas of the house. That way she could stop pretending she was okay and could cry in peace. She'd been awake most of the night, likely because of how much she'd slept at the hospital, and she hadn't slept much this morning, either. More than anything, she just wanted this terrible pain of hers to go away. And she wasn't talking about physical pain—she was referring to emotional suffering.

It was strange how she'd finally been able to stop worrying about her cancer diagnosis, but she hadn't been able to find peace about her and Keith's separation. She didn't want to love a man who had humiliated her in every possible way, but she did. If she could help it, she would, because she certainly wasn't proud of it. Lauren was her best friend and

Jackson was her own flesh and blood, but she was ashamed about the way she was feeling. She couldn't imagine how stupid they must have thought she was; how insane she must be for still wanting her awful husband to leave his mistress and come home. Celine knew there was a chance Lauren and her brother were thinking this way about her, because she'd think the same thing about any other woman in her shoes. She wished she could say she wouldn't, but she was already guilty of doing this kind of thing in the past. Now, of course, she felt bad because she finally knew how "being stupid" actually felt. It was horrible, and at this very moment, Celine remembered and ate every word she'd said about one of her church members—a kind woman who'd cried for months about a husband who'd left her with two small children. The man had even moved into his mistress's home and flaunted her around town like he was single. He'd disrespected his wife on every level, yet the woman had begged and pleaded with him to come back home. She'd forgiven him, and she'd wanted him back, and today, Celine understood it.

Celine reached toward the nightstand and lifted the phone from its base. She dialed Keith's number and waited. To her surprise, he answered.

"Hello?"

"Keith, why didn't you return any of my calls? I tried you three days in a row."

"I've been busy."

"Don't you even care how my surgery turned out?"

"I'm assuming since you're calling me from the home phone, it went well."

"And that's all you have to say about it?"

"What do you want me to say, Celine?"

"I don't know. Anything."

"Look, I can't really talk right now."

"Keith, that's fine if you don't care about me, but what about Kassie? Are you ever planning to call her again or come see her?"

"Of course I am."

"When?"

"Soon. I really have to go, okay? You take care," he said.

Celine held the phone for a whole minute before finally setting it back on the nightstand. She curled her body in the fetal position and sobbed like a child. She'd so thought she was in a better place when it came to Keith, but now that her surgery was over, she felt alone and rejected. Even with Jackson, Lauren, and Kassie there with her, she felt depressed, and she knew it was because of how badly Keith had treated her. She'd asked herself this before, but what she still didn't get was why Keith had done what he'd done, and why now. Why not a year ago or many months from now, when she wasn't dealing with cancer? And he'd been so mean to her before moving out. Then, to add insult to injury, he didn't even want to talk to her or Kassie. Not on his worst day would Celine have expected something like this from Keith. From the time she'd met him, she'd seen him as the ideal husband, and it hadn't taken much at all for her to fall in love with him. He'd been considerate, caring, and responsible, and their marriage had been the one thing Celine had always counted on. She'd known that even if all else failed in life, she and Keith would have each other. She'd believed it was the two of them and their daughter against the world forever.

She lay there, but when she heard someone knocking, she hurried to dry her face with her hands.

"Come in."

Jackson walked over to the bed and sat on the side of it. "What's wrong? Are you hurting? What can I get you?"

Celine thought about the way she'd cried in the recovery room yesterday and how her nurse had thought she was in physical pain, too.

"I'm okay."

"Then why are you crying? And I can tell you've been crying a lot."

"It's nothing."

"Look, Sis, I know this isn't my business, and I'm not trying to hurt your feelings, but if Keith was low enough to leave you like this, you're probably better off without him."

Jackson's comment made Celine weep more.

"I'm sorry, but if that fool doesn't realize what a good woman you are and all he's giving up, then so be it. I know this doesn't feel good, but you're going to have to move on. You're going to have to be strong and find your new normal."

Celine kept quiet because she was too embarrassed to say anything.

"I know it doesn't seem like it now, but you won't always feel this way. It's just going to take some time is all."

"I can't help the way I feel. We've been married for twelve years, Jackson. Keith is the father of my only child. The man I was sure I'd grow old with. So how do I just up and stop loving him?"

"I don't think you can. I don't think anyone could do that when they've loved someone for so long. But I do think you have to see Keith for who he is."

"That's easy to say when you've never been married. It's just not that simple."

"Maybe not, but he just up and moved out like you and Kassie didn't matter. Like you never mattered to him all these years."

"I don't think that's it. Keith and I loved each other, but then my business started taking up a lot of my time."

"That might be true, but Keith's a grown man who knows marriages aren't perfect. Yet he went out and did whatever he wanted."

Celine heard the door opening again, and she was glad to see Lauren. Celine loved her brother, but she couldn't deal with him right now. She heard all that he was trying to tell her, but ultimately he was on the outside looking in, and he had no idea what this was like for her.

"No matter what, though, I want you to remember this," Jackson said. "I love you, and I'll do anything for you. All you have to do is ask."

"I love you, too," she said.

Jackson got up from the side of the bed. "I'm going to check on Kassie. Knowing my little niece, she's glued to some e-reader. But her uncle is going to find some game to beat her at."

Lauren laughed and sat where Jackson had been sitting.

Celine was glad her brother was going to spend time with Kassie, because she definitely didn't want her to come back into the room and see her like this.

"So how are you feeling?" Lauren asked Celine. "You still not hungry?"

"No, not really. Maybe later."

Celine had the comforter pulled up to her chest, but Lauren rested her hand on Celine's leg. "And this too shall pass. I know you're dealing with a lot, but just like you turned your cancer and surgery over to God, you're going to have to do the same thing about your marriage."

"I know, but it just hurts so much," Celine said as tears filled her eyes again. "And it's not getting any better."

"But it will in due time."

"This just doesn't seem real. It's more like a nightmare."

"I can imagine. Not to mention, it's all still very new. Keith has only been gone a week, and you're still grieving. So please don't feel bad about that."

"But I do. I feel crazy for still wanting to be with him."

"Well, you shouldn't. And you definitely don't need

to apologize to anyone about your marriage. That's between you, Keith, and God. Plus, everyone handles love and loss differently. I learned this very thing when David hurt me the way he did. There were moments when I thought it was the end of the world, and I'm sure some people would have called me pathetic. Most people would have just told me to move on and get over it. But eventually, I did that on my own when I was mentally ready. And you will, too."

Celine listened, but no matter what Jackson and Lauren said, all she wanted was her life back. She wanted her husband to come home, so that they could return to living the life they once had. Not just for her, but for Kassie, too. More than anything, Celine wanted to go to sleep, wake up, and discover that none of this had happened.

Two Months Later

Chapter 18

Lauren truly was Celine's best friend forever. As if taking off the entire first week after Celine's surgery so she could care for her and Kassie hadn't been enough, Lauren had now made arrangements with her employer to work only half days in the afternoon for the next two weeks. That way she could take Celine to her last ten radiation treatments. Celine hadn't wanted her to make such a huge sacrifice, especially with her recently being promoted to senior project manager, but while Celine had driven herself to the hospital each day for the first four weeks, she was now highly fatigued. She'd known that exhaustion was a common symptom of radiation, but she'd been hoping it wouldn't happen to her. Of course, once Lauren had found out how tired she was, she'd told Celine she would drive her for as long as Celine needed her to. The good news was that Jackson was flying back in toward the end of next week, so he could take her to one or two treatments also.

But, yes, Lauren had been a sweetheart since day

one, and just thinking about all that she'd done for Celine and Kassie made Celine teary-eyed. That first whole week after surgery, Celine had buried herself into a very dark place, and it had been Lauren who had given her the moral support she'd needed. Celine had cried on and off, daily, over Keith, but she was happy to say that she'd prayed her way out of misery. At one point, she'd slipped into total despair, but then one day she'd woken up feeling different. She hadn't felt sad or hopeless, and she'd finally found the strength to accept Keith's decision. Kassie still had her moments, some of which weren't so great, but Celine knew she could make it as a single parent. It wouldn't be easy, but she felt confident that she and Kassie would be okay. She'd also found a therapist for Kassie, which was helping her a lot, and if it became necessary she would find one for herself.

Celine walked into the radiation room, preparing for her twenty-first treatment. None of them took more than thirty minutes from prep to completion, and Celine was glad of that. This was partly because, beginning with the first treatment, they'd placed ink marks on the exact area of her breast that they wanted to target. They'd done this in order to minimize the effects to surrounding areas, such as her heart, left lung, and arm. They also positioned her very carefully on the table for the same reason. Early on, Celine had wanted to know if she'd lose her hair, and while she knew appearance shouldn't have been important right now, she'd been relieved to learn that she wouldn't.

The story would have been different, though, had she needed to have radiation for something such as a brain tumor, where the rays were directed toward her head. Her radiation oncologist had told her, however, that there was a chance she could lose the hair under her arm. There were other possible risks and side effects, too, but many of them were rare. Celine would have much rather not gone through radiation at all, of course, but she wasn't complaining because her pathology report had returned negative. No cancer had spread to her lymph nodes, and she was thankful.

When Celine's treatment was complete, she and Lauren walked outside and got in Lauren's car. As they left the parking lot, Lauren turned on Kirk Franklin's Praise channel on SiriusXM Radio. Celine took a deep breath and lay back against the headrest.

Lauren looked over at her. "So how are you feeling?"

"I'm really tired, but if it weren't for that I'd be good."

"You'll get your energy back when your treatments are over. So only two more weeks to go."

"I know, I was hoping I wouldn't get tired so quickly, though, because during my first visit, my radiologist told me that fatigue wouldn't likely set in until closer to the end of the six weeks. And I've only done four."

"Yeah, but everyone's body is different. Plus, for a while, you were under a lot of stress."

"Isn't that the truth? But thank you again for doing this."

"Of course, and I know you would do the same for me."

"Without any questions," Celine said, shutting her eyes.

They drove along for about a mile, listening to the radio, and then Lauren said, "So I sort of have something to tell you, and I hope it's going to be okay. We've both wanted to tell you for a while, but we weren't sure how you would feel about it."

Celine opened her eyes and turned toward her. "What's that? And who is 'we'?"

Lauren looked straight ahead at the road. "Jackson and I. We really connected on the day of your surgery. We talked almost nonstop from the time they took you to the operating room until we came to see you in recovery. We talked a lot that evening, too, after you and Kassie went to sleep...and we've talked by phone every single day since then."

Celine raised her eyebrows and smiled at the same time. "Really? Well, isn't that a pleasant surprise."

"Are you serious?"

"Absolutely. My brother is a great guy, and you already know how I feel about you."

Lauren sighed with relief. "Boy, am I glad to hear you say that. We weren't sure if you'd be fine with it or if it might seem strange."

"Not at all, but you wait until I talk to Jackson. What a sneaky little thing he is. You, too, for that matter," she said, and they both laughed.

Just then, however, Celine's cell phone rang, and her stomach stiffened. It was Keith. He hadn't called

Kassie in over a week, which was pretty much the norm for him, and Celine wondered what he wanted.

"I don't believe this," she said, and then answered. "Hello?"

"Hey, how are you?"

"I'm well," she said.

"That's good to hear. I'm glad."

There was an awkward silence until Celine said, "Are you still there?"

"Uh, yeah. Um...hey, I was just wondering if I could stop by to talk to you."

"For what?"

"If you don't mind, I'd rather discuss it when I get there."

"I don't know, Keith. I just finished radiation, and I'm really tired. I was hoping to lie down as soon as I get home."

"I promise it won't take very long."

"Why can't you say whatever you need to say now?"

"I'd really rather talk to you in person."

"Fine. We should be home soon."

"We?"

"Yeah, Lauren and I. She's taking me to my treatments."

"Oh...that's really kind of her. Actually, I wouldn't expect anything different. She's always been a great friend to you."

Celine scrunched her forehead, wondering why Keith was suddenly being so nice. He wanted something, and she couldn't imagine what it might be.

There was just no telling, but more than anything, she hoped he wouldn't be delivering more hurtful news. It was bad enough that he'd left her during the worst time of her life, but for all she knew, he now wanted a divorce. Keith had only been gone nine weeks, but at this point, she wouldn't put it past him. Not when he'd already proven what he was capable of. Not when he hadn't visited or seen Kassie one single time — not when he sometimes went five days or more without as much as calling her or Celine. Nonetheless, Celine would simply have to deal with whatever it was. Good or bad, it was best to get this meeting with Keith done and over.

Chapter 19

"A re you sure you want to do this?" Lauren asked.

Celine nestled further into the sofa in the family room. "Not really, but I also want to hear what he has to say."

"Okay, well, I need to get to work."

"Thank you for everything."

Lauren leaned down and hugged her. "You're welcome, and call me if you need to."

Celine grabbed the TV remote, but then the doorbell rang.

"You want me to let him in?" Lauren said.

"Yeah, if you don't mind."

"I sort of do, but…"

"Try to be cordial," Celine said, chuckling. "Because I know you're not happy with him."

"You can say that again, and I'm surprised he didn't try to use his key."

"I changed the locks, remember? And I told him right after I did it."

"Oh yeah, I forgot about that. Okay, well, I'll see you later."

Lauren went down the hallway, and Celine heard the front door opening. She thought she heard Keith saying hello to Lauren, but she wasn't sure Lauren had responded. When the door shut, Keith made his way into the family room. He could barely look at Celine, and he seemed worried about something.

"Hey," he said, taking a seat across from her and scanning the magazines on the rectangular leather ottoman. He still didn't make eye contact with her.

Celine showed no emotion. "Hi."

"So how are things going?"

"This is my fifth week of treatments, and so far so good."

"How many do you need?"

"Thirty. Remember, I told you that before you moved out."

"Oh yeah, that's right," he said, looking embarrassed and gazing toward the picture window.

Celine wasn't going to make things easy for him, so she stared at him in silence.

He looked at her again. "So, how's Kassie?"

This irritated Celine. "She's doing as well as can be expected for a child who hasn't heard from her own father in more than a week."

"I know, and you have no idea how sorry I am about that. But I have a lot going on."

"Nothing should be more important than your daughter."

"You're right, but I've had a few problems I've had to deal with. Things I wasn't prepared for."

Celine wondered what that meant, but she wasn't about to ask him. She would never let on that she cared one way or the other, so instead she said, "Well, I wasn't *prepared* to take care of our daughter all by myself, either. You claimed you were going to pay child support, but I haven't seen a dime in two months. And it's not like I can pay this mortgage all by myself. So what is it...you don't feel like you're responsible for Kassie any longer?"

"I do, but not living here is part of the reason I wanted to talk to you."

"I'm not sure I understand."

Keith nervously locked his hands together against his abdomen and couldn't seem to get his words out.

Celine was losing her patience. "Keith, why exactly are you here? What is it you want?"

"Okay, okay. The truth is, baby, I made a huge, huge mistake."

"With what?"

"Us, and the way I up and moved out."

Celine knew he had to be joking. "You must be kidding."

"I'm dead serious."

"Really? And what made you realize that?"

"Everything. I don't know what happened to me. I was unhappy, but I never should've started going out all the time, and I never should have left you the way I did."

"Well, what's done is done."

"I know, but I wanna come back home. I love you, and I need you."

Celine was taken aback. These were the very words she'd been hoping to hear from the moment Keith had told her he was leaving. But now nine weeks had passed, and she'd survived a flood of tears, countless sleepless nights, and multiple anxiety attacks. So the idea of letting bygones be bygones and taking Keith back wasn't something she was desperate to do—not anymore. She simply couldn't pretend that he'd been faithful to her when he hadn't. It wasn't like they could go back to the way things were when everything about their marriage had changed.

"Just tell me one thing," she said. "What's so different now versus two months ago?"

"I had a lot of time to think, and it's like I said...I made a huge mistake. Maybe I was going through a midlife crisis. I don't know. But what I do know is that I love you, and I want to come back home. We can get counseling or do whatever you want."

"What about your woman?"

"That's over."

Celine shook her head. "You treated me like an unwanted pet, and now you're saying you made a mistake? And on top of that, you've already stopped seeing this amazing woman who helped break up your marriage? Really, Keith?"

"I know it doesn't make sense, but yes. And I'm sorry. When you kept neglecting me, I got crazy in the head, and I allowed my thoughts and my ego to get the best of me. Then I became reckless and did things I'm ashamed of."

"Well, I'm not sure what to tell you."

"Baby, please," he said, standing up, walking over, and sitting next to her. "I'll do anything you say. If it takes me the rest of my life, I'll make things right. I'll be the kind of husband you deserve from now on."

Celine heard him, but she still couldn't understand where this sudden change of heart was coming from. It didn't make sense, not when he'd been cruel and totally unsympathetic about her feelings and illness. She also thought about his words to her. *"I'm tired of you trying to play the victim...People get sick all the time...They also don't hold pity parties the way you seem to be doing."*

Keith took Celine's hand. "Baby, I'm begging you. If you give me another chance, you won't be disappointed. We'll have an even better marriage than we had before. We'll have a great life together."

Celine pulled her hand away from him. "This is all too much for me right now, and I'd really like you to leave."

"What do I need to do? Just tell me."

"I really want you to go, Keith."

"Okay, I hear you. But please think about everything I've said. I need you to forgive me so we can fix this."

Celine pursed her lips, and Keith finally took the hint and got up.

"I'll check in with you later," he said.

Celine sat on the sofa dumbfounded. To say she was flabbergasted was an understatement.

Chapter 20

Kassie moseyed into the family room and plopped down in a chair. Normally she hugged Celine as soon as she saw her, but not today.

"Hi, honey," Celine said. "How was camp?"

Kassie shrugged her shoulders.

Celine wondered what was bothering her. "Honey, what's wrong? Did something happen?"

"No," she said, looking at the commercial on television.

"Then why do you look like something's wrong? Why do you seem sad?"

Kassie shrugged her shoulders again.

"Look, sweetheart. Whatever it is, you need to tell me."

Kassie looked at her. "Why won't Daddy call me back? Why won't he come see me?"

"Honey, he's probably pretty busy with work."

"But I miss him."

"I know, but it won't always be this way. This is hard for all of us, and it's going to take some getting used to."

"I won't ever get used to Daddy living somewhere else. I want him to come back home and never leave again."

Celine thought about Keith's visit earlier this afternoon, but she couldn't bring herself to tell Kassie about it. Not when it would only give her false hopes.

"I'm sorry this is happening, but for now this is the way things have to be."

"But Mom, I don't want them to be this way. I want us to be a family again. A real family."

Celine wasn't sure what else to say, but it broke her heart to see how down her daughter was. Kassie's therapist had given her another update on Kassie's progress last week, and she'd seemed to be dealing with her parents' separation much better. So maybe she was just having a bad day. Maybe she'd thought about it much more than usual, and the reality of it all was consuming her.

"Why don't you come sit next to me?" Celine said.

"I don't want to!" she shouted.

"Kassie! Since when do you use that kind of tone with me? I know you're upset, but I won't tolerate that."

"I want Daddy to come home."

"I realize that, but it's not going to happen. At least not now, anyway."

"Then when, Mom?"

"I don't know."

"Is it that you won't let him?"

"No, your dad left on his own and you know that."

"But if you asked him to come back, I'll bet he would. He just needs to know it's okay."

"Your dad and I are dealing with some grown-up problems that aren't easy. I know it's hard on you, but I can't do anything to change it right now."

"But you *can* change it. You just have to call him. Tell him you're sorry about whatever you did."

Celine bit her tongue. She had to stop herself from rattling off the truth about Keith. Especially since her daughter had somehow decided to blame her.

"Why is it you think I did something?"

"Because Daddy left. He left us because he wasn't happy, and you both said it wasn't my fault."

"Yes, but this wasn't just about something I did. Sometimes people grow apart. It's unfortunate, sweetheart, but it happens."

"But one time I heard you and Daddy arguing, and he said you cared more about your business than you did about him. He said you never spent time with him."

Celine so wanted to sing like Jennifer Hudson. If she could, she'd tell Kassie how her dad was having an affair with another woman and how he hadn't given Celine one dime of child support since he'd left. But she'd decided weeks ago that no matter how bad things got—no matter how irresponsible Keith continued to be—she would never badmouth him to his daughter. She would keep her mouth shut and allow Kassie to find out the truth on her own terms, even if it wasn't until years from now.

"There's a lot you don't understand, and I think it's best that we talk about something else."

Kassie folded her arms and frowned. "I don't wanna talk about anything else. I just want Daddy to come home."

"You know what? Since you can't seem to get your attitude together and talk to me like I'm your mother, I want you to go upstairs to your room. And stay there until you learn how to show some respect."

Kassie got to her feet and stomped through the family room. Celine had a mind to punish her right then and there, taking away all TV and tablet privileges. But because of the situation, Celine decided to give her the benefit of the doubt—for now.

But as soon as Celine heard Kassie's bedroom door slam shut, the doorbell rang, and Kassie quickly rushed back downstairs.

"I hope that's Daddy," she said, hurrying to the front entrance.

Celine half worried that it might actually be him, but she hoped he wouldn't have the audacity to show up unannounced.

Celine felt too tired to get up, so she didn't. "Make sure you ask who it is before opening the door."

"Auntie Lauren," Celine heard Kassie say, bursting into tears.

"Honey, why are you crying?"

Kassie wept loudly.

"Sweetheart, what's the matter?" Lauren asked.

Celine hated this.

She heard Kassie sniffling and the two of them strolling toward the family room.

"I miss my daddy," Kassie said.

When Lauren and Kassie finally walked in, Lauren had one arm wrapped around Kassie and was holding a white-and-blue paper bag in the other hand. She set the bag down, though, on the arm of the sofa and gave Kassie a full hug.

"Honey, I know this is tough, but you've got to hang in there."

"But Mom won't call Daddy to ask him to come back."

Lauren gazed over at Celine, clearly at a loss for words, and Kassie cried harder.

"I'm so sorry," Lauren said, wiping Kassie's face and picking up the bag she'd set down. "But hey, maybe this frozen custard will make things a little better."

Kassie sniffled a few times. "What kind is it?"

"Your favorite. Vanilla."

Kassie wiped her face with her hands and took the custard into the kitchen.

Celine wasn't in the habit of letting Kassie have sweets before dinner, but she guessed she would make an exception today. Anything to settle Kassie's nerves.

"So how are you feeling?" Lauren said, sitting on the opposite end of the sofa from Celine.

"Still pretty tired."

"Maybe you should go get in bed. Resting on the couch is one thing, but it's not the same."

"I know. Maybe in a little while."

When Celine heard Kassie's bedroom door closing

again, she sighed. "Girl, you just don't know. You couldn't have come at a better time."

"I can tell. And why was Kassie so upset?"

"I don't know. She came home like this."

"I really hate to see her suffering so much."

"I do, too, but before you got here, she was being downright disrespectful."

"Kassie was?"

"Yeah, and you know that's totally unlike her," Celine said.

"Of course it is. But then again, she's never experienced so much pain before."

"She wants her dad to move back home, and somehow she thinks it's my fault that he left."

"She said that?"

"Pretty much."

"What did you tell her?"

"Not a lot, and eventually I sent her to her room."

"Well, what happened when Keith came over? What did he want?"

"Ironically, he wants what Kassie wants."

"Are you serious?"

"Yeah, can you believe that?"

Lauren rested her arm across the back of the sofa. "This from the same man that walked out on you, knowing you had cancer? It's bad enough that he's out there having an affair, but leaving you to fend for yourself while you were sick? That was the worst. Not to mention, he's not doing a thing to help take care of Kassie. It just doesn't get much lower than that."

"I know."

"So what did you tell him?"

"I asked him to leave. I just wanted him to go."

"I don't blame you. He should've thought about that two months ago. I know it's not my place to comment, but I'm really pissed off at Keith for doing this to you. He could have shown you a lot more compassion than he did. He acted as though he couldn't have cared less about you."

Celine knew Lauren was right, and while she couldn't imagine taking Keith back for those very reasons, she also thought about Kassie. If the separation was causing her this much trauma, what would a divorce do? Celine remembered all too well how badly her parents' divorce had affected her many years ago, and she didn't want that for Kassie. Plus, as much as she didn't want to admit it, she still loved Keith. But she also wasn't sure she could ever trust him again. He'd made it clear that he wanted them to reconcile, but she wondered if his betrayal was too much to live with. She worried that their marriage couldn't be saved . . . that it was over for good.

Chapter 21

Kassie rushed into Celine's room ecstatic. "Mom, Mom, Mom!"

It was still early, but Celine sat up in her bed, wondering what all the commotion was about. "Honey, what is it?"

"I just called Daddy, and he told me the great news! He says he wants to come back home, and that he already talked to you about it yesterday!"

Celine wished Keith hadn't told Kassie that, and she knew he'd done it because he hoped Kassie could help encourage Celine's decision.

"I love you so much, Mom," Kassie said, hugging her. "You were going to surprise me, weren't you? That's why you didn't tell me Daddy came over here."

Celine forced a smile on her face, not wanting to disappoint Kassie. "I think we should just talk about this later."

"There's nothing to talk about, Mom. Daddy really wants to come home. He says he misses both of us, and he's really lonely over there all by himself."

Celine didn't say anything, but she couldn't wait to light into Keith for having this kind of conversation with a ten-year-old. All this was doing was making things more awkward for Celine. This would also give Kassie another reason to blame Celine for everything, if she didn't take Keith back the way Kassie wanted.

Celine swung her legs over the side of the bed. "I think you'd better go get in the shower and get dressed. Delia and her mom will be here before you know it."

"Okay, but are you going to call him and tell him it's okay? That way Daddy can start moving his stuff this morning. And he'll be here when I get home from camp."

"Look, sweetheart, it's like I was telling you yesterday. Your dad and I are dealing with some grown-up problems."

"I know, but when he moves back home you can talk about things and make up. Oh please, Mom, please."

Celine didn't have the energy to respond, but that was a mistake because Kassie took her silence to mean something it didn't.

Kassie turned to leave her mom's bedside. "I'm going to go call Daddy right now to let him know you said yes."

"Kassie, no."

Kassie turned around. "Why not?"

"Because your dad and I need to talk."

"Mom, why are you being so mean to Daddy? Don't you still love him?"

"Yes, I do. But that's not the point."

"I don't understand."

"I know you don't, but we're all going to be fine. You'll see."

"I want Daddy to come home."

"Well, what I need you to do now is go take your shower."

Kassie stared at her mom for a few seconds and then stormed out of the room. Celine couldn't get over how unruly her attitude had been since yesterday, and she'd had just about enough of it.

After another hour passed, Kassie reluctantly hugged Celine good-bye and went outside to Sarah's car. She walked as slowly as she could.

Celine stepped outside the front door. "Kassie, it's not like they have all day to wait on you."

Kassie turned and looked back at Celine but didn't walk any faster. It was as if she was trying to be funny. Her actions were rude and defiant. But if she came home with that same attitude this afternoon, Celine would put a stop to it once and for all.

Now, however, she was going to set her husband straight. It was the reason she called him as soon as she went back in the house.

"Hey," he said.

"Hey nothing. Why did you tell Kassie you were over here yesterday, and that you asked to come back home?"

"Because she called me this morning, wanting to know when I would be."

"But you shouldn't have told her that. Not when I never said you could."

"I know, but baby, what was I supposed to say to her? She sounded so upset."

"Yeah, but you had no right telling her anything, because now she won't stop talking about it."

"She really wants us to get back together."

"Well, I'm not ready for that. It took me two months to finally accept that you were gone. That you were never coming back. And now you just want to pretend that none of this ever happened?"

"Baby, I know it's asking a lot, but what about the vows we took?"

Celine raised her eyebrows. "What about them?"

"Don't they mean anything to you?"

"They meant *everything* to me, but apparently nothing to you."

"That's not true. When I married you, I had every intention of being with you until death. I couldn't even imagine a life without you, but things changed. You changed."

"Excuse me?" Celine said.

"Look, baby, please don't get upset. Just hear me out. What I was going to say is you changed, but so did I."

"How did I change, Keith?"

"You stopped having time for me. Before you started your business, our life was near perfect, but then you started working day and night, trying to build up your client list."

"Oh, so because I wanted to better myself, you couldn't handle it?"

"No, but I'll admit that I did like it better when you worked at the hospital."

"But you know that wasn't enough for me. I wanted to do something on my own."

"Yeah, but things changed. You stopped cooking dinner, you were too tired for sex, and we rarely went out anywhere together."

"Well, I'm sorry that you felt neglected, because that wasn't my intent, but that still doesn't justify what you did. Neglect and adultery are two totally different things, and you could have come to me."

"But I did."

"Not really. You just left."

"And I'll always regret that. My actions were rash and quick, and you deserved better than that."

"Exactly, because I never would have done something like this to you. Even if I'd decided I wanted out, I wouldn't have started seeing another man before we got divorced. That's the one thing that makes me sick about people who mess around. If you don't want to be with someone any longer, why not file for a divorce? Why not show the person you're married to a little courtesy? Especially after twelve years."

"Baby, you're absolutely right, and I don't blame you for feeling the way you do. But that still doesn't change the fact that I love you. You're my heart and joy, and I'm sorry I lost faith in that. I lost faith in us, and now I'm paying a huge price for it."

"Well, regardless, I'm asking you to please not discuss our situation with Kassie anymore. This has to stay between you and me."

"Understood."

"I mean it, Keith, and I'll talk to you later."

"Wait. So are you at least considering everything I said to you yesterday? Can we go to counseling? Can I move back home?"

Celine wasn't sure if he was simply being persistent or just didn't get what she was trying to tell him. She didn't want to talk about his moving back in.

"We need more time apart," she said.

"Why? What good is that going to do us?"

"I need time to sort things out."

"Even though our separation is tearing Kassie apart?"

"You can blame yourself for that. You're the one who took the selfish way out. You did what you wanted."

"Baby, what is it going to take?" he asked. "What do I need to do? How do I prove how sorry I am and that I will never, ever do something like this again?"

"I don't know that you *can* prove it."

Keith sighed loudly. "I don't know what else to say. I'm trying my best to fix this."

"I need to go."

"Can I come over so we can talk in person?"

"Lauren will be here soon to take me to the hospital."

"Then what about this afternoon?"

"I don't think so. I'll be tired."

"Baby, please."

"I have to go, Keith. I'll talk to you later," she said, and hung up.

She knew it was rude not to wait for his response, but just thinking about the way he'd treated her made her want to hurt someone. She was only so far from hating him, something she was trying her best not to do, because she knew God wasn't okay with that. She'd also been trying to mask her true rage as much as possible for Kassie's sake, because no matter what, Keith was still Kassie's father. She didn't like that particular fact, but it couldn't be changed and she was doing her best to keep that in mind. Maybe down the road she wouldn't feel so incensed, and she'd be able to forgive Keith. Mostly she just wanted to stop loving a man who had deceived her in the worst way. She simply wanted to be happy and at peace again.

Chapter 22

*T*oday wasn't a good day for Celine. She'd just returned from her radiation treatment, but she was more exhausted than she'd been yesterday. She'd also learned earlier from her blood work results that her hemoglobin level was a tad low, and that the doctor was planning to monitor her closely. He was concerned that she might be slipping into anemia, something that was very common for patients receiving radiation.

Lauren had asked Celine if she wanted her to take the afternoon off to stay with her, but Celine had insisted she go on to work, especially since Celine was already in bed resting, and she would stay there until Kassie got home. She was a little concerned, however, about the light-headedness she was experiencing, so she settled further into her pillow and closed her eyes. That lasted all of two minutes before her phone rang. She had a mind to ignore it, but if for some reason it was Lauren calling and Celine didn't answer, Lauren would be in her car and on her way back to see about her.

Celine picked up her phone and smiled when she saw that it was her brother.

"Hey, baby brother, how are you?"

"The question is, how are you?"

"I'm pretty tired today."

"More than usual?"

"Yeah, it's a lot more noticeable than it has been. But you know my radiologist warned me early on to expect fatigue as one of the side effects."

"Maybe you should go see your surgeon."

"Lauren suggested the same thing earlier, but for right now I'm just going to rest and see how I'm feeling tomorrow. If I feel worse, I'll make an appointment."

"I hope so, because I'm really worried about you. Lauren has been keeping me updated, and I'm starting to feel like I need to get on a plane. I wasn't planning to come until next week, but..."

"No, I'm fine. The last thing I want is for you to miss more work than you have to."

"I have vacation, Sis, so it's not like I won't get paid."

"Yeah, but I don't want you to use all of it for me. It's just not necessary."

"Still trying to boss me, I see," he said.

"Of course," she said, laughing. "I'll be doing that until the end of time."

"Uh-huh, I'm sure you will."

"And, anyway, enough about me. Because you know I'm mad at you, right?"

"About what?"

"Lauren told me about your secret love connection."

Jackson laughed. "She told me last night that she'd finally confessed to you. I just didn't know how to tell you."

"Why?"

"I don't know. I guess I wasn't sure how you would react."

"You sound like Lauren, but I'm really happy for you guys."

"Thanks, Sis. And I'm glad you feel that way, because I think Lauren is the one."

"As in *the* one?"

"Yep."

"Really? Now that's the shocker of the week."

"Yeah, I know, right? I've never believed I would find any woman who was worth giving up my bachelor life for. And while I'd always thought Lauren was gorgeous, I never saw her the way I see her now. Not even when we were kids. But the more we talked the day of your surgery, the more connected I felt to her. The chemistry between us is crazy."

"Well, good for you. And good for Lauren, because you both deserve to be happy."

"She's everything I could ever want in a woman, although I wish I could be the same for her."

"Why do you say that?"

"I don't know. I just wish I had more money saved. If I hadn't taken so long to get my bachelor's, I would have."

"Well, let's be honest, even after you started working, you spent money like there was no tomorrow."

"Can't deny it. I enjoyed myself every chance I got. Then I bought my condo and put a nice amount down on that."

"That was a good investment, though."

"I know, but it still means I don't have a lot of money stashed away. Not in personal savings or retirement."

"But you will. You earn a great salary, and you'll be good. Plus, Lauren isn't like that. She would never hold that against you. What she's always wanted is to have a man love her and be faithful to her."

"Well, I can definitely do that, and I will. I haven't asked her yet, but she's going to be your sister-in-law."

"Oh my goodness, Jack. This is wonderful. You two are going to be very happy."

Jackson paused and then said, "As much as I hate to bring him up, have you heard anything from Keith?"

"I have. Yesterday and today. He wants to move back home."

"What? Please tell me you're joking."

"No, he's very serious."

"Well, I hope you know you can't trust that fool. Any time a man just up and leaves for no legitimate reason, he isn't worth being with."

"I agree, and I've told myself that over and over. But while I was getting my treatment, I kept thinking about Kassie. I've seen a side of her these last couple of days that I've never seen before, and it's all because she wants her dad to come home. She wants us to be a family again, and that makes me feel like I have to at least consider working things out with Keith. I mean, you know what it was like for us when Mom and Dad split up. It was the worst time of our lives. I was never the same after that, and I used to pray daily for them to get back together. I couldn't imagine them being apart, living in separate households, and I hated seeing Dad just on weekends. Then when he started dating, I hated that even more."

"I remember all that, but I also don't believe you should let Keith treat you any way he wants to. He left you for some skank, Sis, so please tell me you're not planning to take that joker back."

"I honestly don't know. I thought I did, but we have a child, Jack. A very hurt child who isn't taking this very well. And if there's one thing I know, it's this: Whatever happens to you as a child, good or bad, affects you for the rest of your life."

"I'm going to say this again. Please tell me you're not planning to take that no-good brother-in-law of mine back."

"I don't want to, but I also took vows before God, and I don't want to end my marriage without knowing I did everything I could to save it."

Jackson sighed in disgust. "I'm telling you now, the man can't be trusted. He's already proven that in more ways than one. I'll tell you something else, too. He'd better be glad he never showed his face while I was in town."

Celine wished Jackson would calm down, but just

as she was about to tell him to do so, her doorbell rang.

"Hey, someone's at the door, so I'll call you later, okay?"

"I hope that's not him."

"Good-bye, Jack. I love you."

"This conversation isn't over, but I love you, too."

Celine got herself out of bed, but she felt weak and light-headed again. Still, she walked down the stairs and through the hallway and looked out the front door. She shook her head when she saw Keith standing there with what looked like at least two dozen roses. She had a mind to walk away, but she opened the door. When she did, however, her head became heavy, and she felt dizzy. Seconds later, she collapsed on the floor.

Chapter 23

Celine blinked the blurriness from her eyes and looked around to see what all the fuss was about. She heard a siren whistling in the background and a man saying that an IV was already being started. She didn't hear anyone respond, so she wasn't sure who he was talking to.

She blinked a few more times, and then she looked slightly upward and saw a man in uniform. When she looked in front of her, she saw Keith. At the same time, she noticed something covering her face. This was when she panicked.

"Baby, it's okay," Keith said, rubbing her arm. "We're in the ambulance, and we're almost at the hospital. Please try to stay calm."

Celine wondered what had happened to her and why she was being rushed to the ER. She tried to remember something—anything—but she couldn't.

"I'm here, baby," Keith said, "and I'm not going anywhere."

Suddenly Celine realized how groggy she was, but

she heard the paramedic talking to someone again. He wasn't speaking to Keith, though, so maybe it was to a doctor.

Keith caressed her hair. "Hang in there, baby. I love you so much, and I won't leave your side, no matter what."

Celine gazed at him, and while she didn't say anything, she was glad to have him there. As of this moment, she didn't care about what Keith had done or what the current state of their marriage was. She was just happy to have someone there with her—her husband looking out for her the way he was supposed to. It was also then that she remembered the doorbell ringing and how when she'd opened the door for Keith he'd been holding flowers. It must have been then that she'd passed out.

Celine raised her hand to remove the oxygen mask, but Keith stopped her.

"Try not to talk. We're almost there. You're gonna be fine."

Celine watched him for a few more seconds and then closed her eyes. Before long, they arrived in front of the ER entrance, and the paramedics removed her from the ambulance and wheeled her inside. At the direction of a medical staff member, they rolled her down to her designated examination room and transferred her onto a hospital gurney.

"Good luck, ma'am," the paramedic who'd been in the back of the ambulance with her said.

Keith shook his hand. "Thank you for everything.

Thank you as well," he said, turning to the driver and shaking his hand also.

"I'm Dr. Cates," the attending physician said to Celine, and she saw two nurses, one typing information into the computer and the other connecting her to various hospital monitors.

The doctor moved closer to Celine. "I'm going to remove your oxygen mask, but you let me know if you feel like you're having shortness of breath."

Celine shook her head and waited. Thankfully, she felt fine.

"Can you breathe okay?" Dr. Cates asked.

"Yes."

"Good. So, while you were en route, we checked your patient file and see that you're in the midst of having daily radiation."

"I am."

"And your hemoglobin has been dropping a little as well."

"Yes."

"That may be the problem, but I'm ordering a full blood workup to see if we can figure out exactly what's going on. If your hemoglobin has dropped a lot lower, that would also explain your low blood pressure and your resting heart rate, which is very high."

Celine took a deep breath and silently prayed. *Lord, please take care of me. Protect me.* Then she silently recited Matthew nine, twenty-two, the same as Lauren had told her to do before she'd had surgery. *Daughter, be encouraged! Your faith has made you well.*

When Dr. Cates left, the younger nurse with coal-black hair confirmed the correct spelling of Celine's name and her birthdate. Then she snapped a plastic ID bracelet around Celine's wrist.

"Are you in any pain?" the older nurse asked her.

"No, I'm not. I just feel really tired."

"Well, hopefully they'll figure out what's causing that very soon. Someone from the lab should be in shortly, but in the meantime, just let us know if you need anything. Your call light is right there," she said, pointing to it, "and you can also control the television from there as well."

"Thank you," Celine said.

The older nurse smiled. "You're quite welcome."

When both women left, Keith took a seat in the chair at the side of the bed and grabbed Celine's hand. Celine looked at him and saw tears in his eyes.

"Baby, I am so sorry I wasn't here for you when you had surgery. I'm sorry for everything, and I know I was wrong. I have a lot of making up to do, and I'll do that if you'll just let me come back home. Let me take care of you."

Celine gazed into his eyes but didn't speak.

"I can't lose you," he continued. "Not over my crazy, heartless mistake. All I want is to spend the rest of my life with you. The way I promised I would years ago."

Celine still didn't comment and finally looked away from him.

"Baby, just tell me what to do. I'm willing to do anything. But please don't make me lose my family. You and Kassie are all I have, and we both owe Kassie a chance at growing up with two parents."

Celine was glad Keith was there because she was afraid to be left alone, but she didn't want to talk about their marriage. Not right now.

"Keith, I'm really tired."

"Baby, I know, and I'm sorry to keep bothering you with this, but I just want you to know how much I love you and how sorry I am."

Celine closed her eyes, and Keith didn't say anything else.

But then she opened them again. "Hey, can you do me a favor and call Lauren?"

"Of course," Keith said. "What's her number?"

Celine recited it, and after Keith punched the digits into his phone, he passed it over to her.

"Hello?" Lauren said.

"Hey, girl, it's me."

"Is everything okay? Where are you?"

"I'm at the emergency room."

"Oh no, what happened?"

"I passed out, and they're going to run a few blood tests."

"I'll be there as soon as I can."

"You don't have to do that. Since my cell phone is at home, I didn't want you to call and not get an answer."

"That's why I asked where you were. I didn't recognize the hospital's phone number."

"I'm actually calling you from Keith's phone."

"Oh really? How did that come about?"

"Long story."

"I'll see you shortly."

"I really don't want you to leave work. It's not that serious, and I'll call you when I know what's going on."

"Come on, now. You know I'm not hearing any of that."

Celine sighed and slightly chuckled. "I'll see you soon, girl."

Keith took his phone back. "So is Lauren on her way?"

"Yeah."

"She's been a very good friend to you, and I really need to thank her for that. She was there for you when I wasn't."

Celine wished he wouldn't keep reminding her of that, because it was only making her angry.

Keith leaned back in the chair. "Gosh, I really messed up, but I'm here now and I won't ever disappoint or hurt you again," he said, caressing her arm.

Celine wasn't sure how to feel about Keith, and that bothered her. She knew there was no way she should as much as entertain the idea of taking Keith back, but she couldn't help thinking about what he'd said not long ago: "*We both owe Kassie a chance at growing up with two parents.*" Then she thought about how upset Kassie had been this morning when she'd learned her father wanted to return home and Celine hadn't said he could. Celine was terribly confused and unsure about everything—all while laid up in the emergency room, wondering why she'd collapsed in her entryway. She hoped it was nothing serious and that she'd be able to go home in a few hours. She prayed that God would fix every aspect of her life and guide her decisions. Because she certainly had a lot of them to make. Could she actually take back a man who'd walked out on her for another woman? Could she ever trust him again? And if it turned out that she couldn't trust him, should she force herself to stay married to Keith for Kassie's sake?

Celine closed her eyes, tossing a number of thoughts through her mind. But it wasn't long before they turned toward the woman Keith had slept with. For some reason, Celine hadn't asked him more than a few questions about her, and even those questions hadn't been specific. But suddenly Celine wanted to know everything: the woman's name, what she looked like, where she worked, where she lived, if she had children, where she'd been born, if she had an ex-husband, did she attend church, etc., etc., etc. Most of all, though, Celine wanted to know what this tramp of a woman had that she didn't. What was it that had been so great about her? What had this woman done to convince Keith to move out of his own house, abandoning his wife and daughter? Yet now he was begging like a child to move back in? Not to mention, he'd only been gone for two months, and now this woman was already out of the picture? Celine wasn't sure what to think or how things were going to turn out between them, but she wanted answers. She wanted the truth and nothing less than that.

Chapter 24

eline was glad to be home. It had taken Dr. Cates a little longer than he'd thought to get her results back, but once he had, he'd informed her that she was slightly anemic. She wasn't to the point where she needed a blood transfusion, but Dr. Cates had explained that if Celine didn't take it easy, she would. The doctor had also prescribed her some iron pills to take until she was better.

Lauren pulled the comforter closer to Celine's shoulders, and Keith stood at the side of the bed with his arms crossed. Since he'd ridden to the hospital with Celine by ambulance, he'd had to catch a ride back with Lauren—and he hadn't said one word the entire trip. He knew Lauren no longer liked him, and he was trying to tread lightly around her. Kassie, who they'd picked up from Delia's on the way home, sat very close to her mom on the bed.

Lauren placed the remote control on the nightstand so that Celine could easily access it. Then she reminded Celine of the doctor's instructions. "You do remember what Dr. Cates said, right? No caffeine, drink plenty of water, but more than anything else, he wants you to get as much rest and sleep as possible and make sure you stand up slowly when you've been sitting or lying down for an extended period of time."

"Yes, Mother," Celine said, smiling.

"Okay, you're joking, but you really need to take care of yourself. You've got to take it easy until you finish up your treatments."

"I will. I promise."

Kassie looked concerned. "So, Mom, are you going to be okay?"

"Of course."

"Are you going to have to go back to the hospital again?"

"You mean for my treatments?"

"No, like you did tonight. And will they make you spend the night next time?"

"I hope not."

"I hope not, too. I don't want you to have to stay there."

"Well, either way, I don't want you worrying about me. All right?"

"I can't help it, Mom. I was really afraid when Auntie Lauren called Delia's mom and said you were at the hospital. I thought something really bad was going to happen."

Celine smiled. "I know it must have frightened you, but as you can see I'm doing fine."

"Are you still tired? Because you look really tired, Mom."

"I am, but the doctor gave me some medicine to help that."

"I hope it works."

"So do I. But you know what else?"

"What?"

"It's almost your bedtime."

"Awww, Mom. Can't I stay in here with you just a little while longer?"

"I wish you could, but it's already pretty late."

"Okay," she said, standing up.

"Now, give me a hug," Celine told her.

"Good night, Mom," she said.

"Good night, sweetie."

As Kassie walked past her father, he touched the top of her head. "I'll be in shortly so you can say your prayers, and I can tuck you in."

"Okay, Daddy," she said, hugging him.

When Kassie left, Keith turned back to Celine. "Do you need me to do anything for you?"

"No, but I really appreciate you calling an ambulance and then staying with me at the hospital. It's a good thing you left work and came by when you did."

"It was no problem, and if you want I can spend the night."

Lauren hurried to speak up. "I've already got that covered. Plus, I'm taking Celine in for her radiation in the morning, anyway."

Keith didn't respond, but he looked at Celine.

"I'm good, Keith. Lauren is staying, so I know I'll be okay."

Keith paused before leaving the room. He seemed to want to make his case, but he didn't.

When he was gone, Lauren rolled her eyes. "He can't be serious. He actually thought you were going to let him spend the night?"

"I guess so. And he talked a lot about moving back home again, too. That's mostly all he talked about until you arrived at the hospital."

Now Lauren sat on the side of Celine's bed. "Look, girl. I know this is none of my business, and that you're a grown woman, but please be careful."

"I am."

"I mean, I don't ever want to tell any woman to divorce her husband, but Keith was wrong and he knows it. When you really needed him, he was nowhere to be found."

"I know."

"And now he's all of a sudden hanging around, pleading with you to take him back?"

Celine agreed with everything Lauren was saying, but she couldn't help thinking about Kassie. She'd also be lying if she said she wasn't terrified of becoming a single mom. It wasn't the kind of life she'd signed up for, and she also knew she couldn't afford to pay all the household bills without Keith's income. She'd had no problem paying them for the last two months, but in another three or four, much of her savings would be gone—including her retirement account, since she'd used most of that to start her business. If she and Keith divorced and he paid her regular child support, she and Kassie might be able to get by, but they would still struggle to make ends meet. She just wouldn't have enough to cover the mortgage, utilities, and general home maintenance all by herself. She also wouldn't be able to shop for groceries the way she'd always done or buy certain things Kassie was used to getting.

But even if Celine pushed her potential financial woes to the side, there was something else that troubled her. No matter how callously Keith had treated her—no matter how he'd betrayed her love and trust, no matter how he'd slept with another woman behind her back—she still loved him. Regardless of how hard she tried to stop, she couldn't seem to do it. Keith was her husband and Kassie's father, and Celine wasn't sure how to get beyond this. Should she swallow her pride and stay with Keith or file for divorce as soon as possible? She'd eventually have to make a decision, one way or the other, as there was simply no getting around it.

Chapter 25

*L*auren drove in front of Celine's house and saw Keith parked in the driveway, sitting in his SUV. Lauren and Celine were just returning from her treatment appointment.

Celine could only imagine what Lauren was about to say.

"What is he doing here?" she asked. "Shouldn't he be at work?"

"As far as I know."

"He's really something else," Lauren said, pulling in next to him. But before she could unbuckle her seat belt, Keith jumped out of his vehicle, hurried around to the passenger side of Lauren's vehicle, and opened the door for Celine. He helped her out of the car, placed his arm around her waist, and escorted her up to the front door.

When they got inside, Lauren followed behind them and set Celine's purse next to her on the family room sofa. "Can I get you anything?"

Celine shook her head. "No, I think I'm good for now."

Keith moved closer to Lauren. "Look, I know you're not happy about me being here, but I'm really sorry about what I've done. And I'm trying to make up for it."

Lauren barely looked at him. "You don't owe me any explanations at all."

"I know, but you're Celine's best friend and I wanted you to know that," he said, then turned to Celine. "And baby, I want you to know that I've taken a leave of absence from work. That way, I can take you to the rest of your treatments and be here with you around the clock."

Celine was shocked but showed no emotion. She wasn't sure what to think about any of what he was saying. He'd gone from not caring one bit about her cancer diagnosis to now taking unpaid time off from his job?

"I think I'd better go so the two of you can talk," Lauren said.

"Thank you for everything," Celine said. "I owe you so much."

Lauren leaned down and hugged her. "I've told you this at least a thousand times: You don't owe me anything. All I want is for you to get well."

"I really appreciate you."

"Anytime, and I'll call you later," Lauren said.

Celine relaxed against the sofa pillow. "Keith, don't you think you should have asked me first?"

"Asked you what?"

"Whether I wanted you to take a leave of absence. Whether I want you spending all your time here and taking me to my radiation treatments."

"I just assumed you would. Especially since it would prevent Lauren from having to miss any more work. Plus, baby, I'm your husband, and it's my responsibility."

"It was *always* your responsibility. But you chose to leave me instead."

"I know, and I'll always be ashamed of what I did and how I did it. But it's like I told you before, I made a huge mistake."

"You did more than that. You hurt me like no one else ever has in my life, and you humiliated me. You made up some lame excuse as to why you wanted out, and you left Kassie and me like we didn't matter."

Keith sat down next to her with an aura of sadness. "I know, and it was a sick and awful thing to do. It's as though I lost my mind for a while."

Celine was starting to feel tired again, but she wasn't heading up to bed until Keith told her everything she wanted to know.

"So what's this woman's name?"

"Who?"

Celine stared at him as though he were crazy.

"Oh," he said. "Paulette Wilson."

"What does she look like?"

Keith seemed uncomfortable. "She's average height, about a size ten, and she has short hair."

"That's interesting."

"Why?"

"Because I'm tall with shoulder-length hair."

"Baby, do we really have to do this?"

"Yeah, Keith, as a matter of fact we do. So where does she work?"

"She's a hairstylist."

"Does she own her own salon?"

"No."

"Does she go to church?"

"Not really." .

"Either she does or she doesn't."

"She only goes once or twice a year."

"Does she have any children?"

"Two."

"Boys or girls?"

"One of each."

"How old?"

"Two and eight."

"Do they have the same father?"

"No."

"Was she married to either of them?"

"Both."

"Is she from here?"

"No, she's from Charlotte."

Celine wasn't sure why, but for some reason, she was relieved to learn what she had about this woman. It didn't lessen the hurt or diminish how wrong Keith had been for having an affair, but at least some of Celine's curiosity had been met—but not all of it.

"There's something else I want to know."

"What's that?"

"What was so special about her? What does she have that I don't?"

Keith stared directly into Celine's eyes. "To be honest, she couldn't hold a single candle to you if she tried. She's not nearly as beautiful as you are, and you're a hundred times smarter than her. You've also been blessed with the kind of class she'll never have. She could never fully compare to you, period. But there was one thing I couldn't ignore."

"Which was what?"

"She was willing to do any and everything I asked her to do. From day one, she went out of her way to please me and make me happy. She said she would always make sure I never felt alone . . . the way I had with you."

"Well, if that's true, then why are you here?"

"Because after a while, I knew I'd made a mistake. I knew I didn't love her, and that I could never love any woman the way I love you."

Celine didn't have words, so she stood up. "I'm ready to lie down."

"Baby, is that all you have to say?"

"I want you to leave."

"You're too weak to be here all alone."

"I can take care of myself."

"Well, at least let me help you upstairs."

"No! I want you out of here!"

"Baby, please give me a chance. Please let me be here for you."

Celine held on to the back of the sofa. "Just leave."

"Okay, if that's what you want, but I'm calling Lauren," he said.

"No. Don't you call anybody. I'll be fine."

Keith opened his mouth to speak again, but he obviously changed his mind, because he turned and walked out of the room. Before long, Celine heard the front door opening and shutting.

It was then that she made her way back around the sofa, dropped down on it, and cried like someone had died.

Chapter 26

*C*eline flipped her bedroom television between *CBS This Morning*, *Good Morning America*, and the *Today* show. This was one of those mornings when they each had various segments she wanted to see, and she was trying to catch them all.

When a commercial came on, Kassie walked into the room and got in bed with her. She still had on her pajamas, but it wouldn't be long before it was time for her to get ready.

"So when is Daddy moving back home? I just got off the phone with him, and he says he can't come back until you say he can. Is that true, Mom?"

Celine had so been hoping Kassie wouldn't bring this up again. At least not for a while. "It's a complicated situation, and I'm sorry for the way our separation is hurting you."

"But all you have to do, Mom, is let him come back. Please, Mom. Pretty, pretty please."

"I'm sorry."

"Mom, don't you want us to be happy?"

"It's nothing like that."

"Well, just call him and tell him to come back," she said, reaching for the phone on the nightstand and passing it to Celine.

"Look, Kassie. I'm done talking about this for now."

"But Mom—"

Celine frowned. "I mean it, Kassie. I'm done, and I don't want to hear another word about this."

Kassie burst into tears, crying loudly. "Well, if Daddy can't come back home, I don't want to live anymore. I want to die like your mommy and daddy did."

Celine pressed the Mute button on the remote and tossed it onto the bed. "I want you to stop this nonsense, right now!" she shouted. "You hear me, Kassie? And I'd better not ever hear you say something like that again."

Kassie cried harder, but this time she hugged Celine. "I'm so sorry, Mom. I...didn't...mean...it. I... just...want...Daddy...to...come...back...home," she said, sniffling.

"I understand that, but when I say we're done talking about something, I mean it."

"I just want you and Daddy to love each other again. I don't want to live at two houses the way some of the kids at summer camp do. Some of the kids at my school have to do that, too, and they hate their parents for breaking up. It's just not fair, Mom, because I still love you and Daddy both. I'll always love you."

"Honey, I know, and I'm sorry. I can't apologize enough."

"But can't you at least try to love Daddy again?"

"Sweetheart, I've never stopped, but that's not the problem."

"He loves us, too, and he says he won't ever leave us again. Not ever."

Celine wasn't happy about the way Keith continued to speak to Kassie as though she were an adult. He had no right talking to her about their marital problems, but Celine knew he was doing it on purpose. He was still playing on Kassie's sympathy, hoping it would somehow affect Celine's decision. The sad thing was, it was slightly working. After crying profusely yesterday afternoon, Celine had found herself weighing her options. Part of her wanted to end things with Keith for good and file for divorce, but part of her wanted to keep her family together. She also wanted to do what she believed God wanted all married couples to do—honor their vows and work out their differences. He wanted them to love and forgive each other the way He forgave all of His children. This was the hard part for Celine, though. Forgiving in spite of the way she truly felt. Trying to move on and forget the way Keith had treated her. Trying to accept that Keith had sought out another woman, committed adultery, and acted as though Celine's illness wasn't serious. He'd done enough to last a lifetime, more than most women could stomach, yet Celine sat there teetering back and forth.

But then Kassie looked at her with more tears flowing down her face. "Mom, if you won't do it for Daddy, can you please do it for me? I just don't wanna be sad anymore. I don't want my heart to keep hurting. It hurts really bad. So please, Mom, can he come back?"

Celine still wasn't sure what to do, but seeing her daughter in such heart-wrenching pain was too much. Kassie hadn't done a thing to deserve this, and if taking her father back would make her happy, Celine was willing to make the sacrifice. Very few people would understand her decision, but this wasn't about everyone else. This was about her daughter's happiness, and Celine had to make that her priority. She had to focus on Kassie's state of mind and overall well-being, and that was all that mattered.

Chapter 27

*H*ours had passed, yet Celine still wasn't feeling very energized. She'd also discovered this morning that even though she was taking her iron medication, her iron level had dropped below what it had been at the ER. All she wanted was to feel better, physically and mentally, but while it was two in the afternoon, she felt like lying down and taking a nap.

And she would have, if she hadn't already called Keith to come over. Earlier this afternoon, she'd debated her decision once again, but now he was sitting in front of her at the kitchen island, waiting to hear what she had to say.

"So these are the ground rules. There won't be any sleeping together in the same room, and no sex under any circumstances. Then, once my radiation treatments are finished and I have more strength, I want us to go to marital counseling."

"Of course. Whatever you want."

"And if...and I do mean *if*...things get better for

us, I still won't be having sex with you until we've both been tested for HIV."

"That won't be a problem."

"Nonetheless, I need you to understand how things are going to work from now on."

"I told you I would do anything you ask, and I meant that."

"I'm glad you feel that way, because the other thing I want is for you to call this Paulette person to let her know things are over between the two of you for good. I want you to tell her that you're moving back home and to never contact you again."

"No worries," he said. "I already ended things with her."

"That's fine, but I want to hear you tell her with my own ears."

Keith squinted his eyes. "Don't you think that's being a little childish?"

"Call it whatever you want, but either you call her in front of me, or all bets are off."

"She's at work right now."

"Then you can do it this evening once Kassie goes to bed."

Keith nodded in agreement, but Celine could tell he didn't want to do it. And it wasn't like he had to, either. However, if he didn't do everything she requested, he wouldn't be moving back home, not even for Kassie. This morning Celine had made up her mind to do what was best for their daughter, but when she'd awakened from her nap a couple of hours ago, she'd decided that Keith would do things her way or no way at all. It was the only answer in terms of eliminating unnecessary stress—the kind of stress she couldn't continue to have and stay in remission.

When Kassie finished saying her prayers, she hugged and kissed both of her parents and got in bed. "Good night, Mom. Good night, Daddy. I'm so happy now," she said, smiling more than Celine had seen her smile in weeks.

"We're so glad to hear that, sweetheart," Keith said. "Now you get some sleep, okay?"

"Okay. I love you, Daddy."

"I love you, too."

"I love you, Mom."

"I love you more."

Keith followed Celine out of Kassie's room, shutting the door behind them.

"So are you heading to bed, or do you want me to stay awhile longer?" he asked.

"No, I want us to go downstairs so you can make your phone call."

Keith immediately looked uncomfortable, the same as he had earlier, but Celine started down to the kitchen and so did he. It was best to do it there because that way Kassie wouldn't hear anything.

He pulled his phone from his jacket, which was lying on the chair, and dialed the number. He hung up fairly quickly, though. "She's not answering."

"Well, if you don't get her tonight, then tomorrow."

"Not a problem. And hey, how many more treatments do you have?"

"One tomorrow and the final five next week."

"That's really great to hear. So can I take you to those? I mean, that is the reason I took a leave of absence."

"I guess. I'll call Lauren tonight to let her know she doesn't need to pick me up in the morning."

"Good. And baby, thank you for not giving up on me," he said. "Thank you for giving me a chance."

Celine didn't respond, but just then, Keith's phone rang.

"Is that her?"

Keith looked at his screen. "Yeah."

"Then answer it."

He hesitated but then finally pressed the Send button.

"Hello?" he said, obviously thinking he was about to have a quick one-on-one conversation...until Celine reached for his phone and placed it in speaker mode.

"Did you hear me?" Paulette spat.

"No, I didn't," he said.

"I asked why you were calling me."

Celine could tell the woman was irritated.

"I need to say a couple of things," he told her.

"Like what?"

"I can't see you anymore. My wife and I are getting back together, and I'm moving back home."

"Excuse me? And you're telling me this why? Oh, wait a minute. Is this some production you're putting on for your little wifey? Am I on speaker? Well, if so, did you tell her I dumped you more than a week ago, right after you got fired?"

"What?" Celine said louder than she'd planned. "Keith, what is she talking about?"

"Oh my goodness," Paulette said, laughing. "So you didn't tell her you got fired for sleeping with one of your coworkers? And that the little tramp is filing a sexual harassment lawsuit against you and the company?"

Celine felt like she was about to pass out again. She must have been dreaming. Had to be.

"You've got some nerve calling me, Keith," Paulette said. "Pretending like you broke up with me when you know I ended things as soon as I found out what you were up to. And sweetheart," she said, obviously speaking to Celine, "make no mistake about it, this ratchet husband of yours is only trying to get back with you because he can't afford to live on his own anymore."

Celine sighed. "Keith, is all of this true? Meaning your whole leave-of-absence story was a lie?"

Keith pressed the End button on his phone. "Baby, there's a lot more to the story. So please let me explain."

"More to the story? What more could there possibly be? I heard that tramp of yours, loudly and clearly. You've been sleeping with two different women, and now you don't have a job."

"I know, baby, but that chick at work is lying. She came after *me*."

Celine raised both of her hands in front of her. "Just get out, Keith, and this time stay out."

"Baby, no. Please don't do this," he begged, but it was what happened next that broke Celine's heart.

"Daddy, who was that lady on the phone?" Kassie asked. She stood inside the doorway between the kitchen and the corridor, and both Celine and Keith turned around in horror.

"Did you really lose your job, Daddy?"

"Oh no," Celine whispered, moving toward her daughter and hugging her. "Honey, let's go back upstairs."

"Daddy, who was that lady on the phone? And why was she saying you slept with your coworker?"

Keith walked closer to them. "Honey, that never happened. The woman on the phone was lying."

Celine nudged Kassie toward the hallway, and they went upstairs. Celine couldn't believe how stupid she'd been. She'd actually given in and made the decision to take Keith back, only to learn that he'd been sleeping with not one, but two other women. And who was to say there weren't more of them? There was no telling what else he'd done and what more Celine would find out as time went on. Then there was this news about his losing his job and the fact that he was being sued.

It was this last thought that stirred her nerves into a frenzy. "Oh my God," she said out loud to herself while holding her daughter in her arms, trying to console her. If Keith had been fired, how in the world was she going to pay all her medical bills? More important, how would she and Kassie survive? What was going to happen to them now?

Epilogue

Six Weeks Later

*C*eline's cancer was fully in remission, but here she was back in the ER again. This time she wouldn't be leaving for a few days, as the doctor had just informed her that her hemoglobin level was only 6.5—life-threateningly low—and she needed a blood transfusion. Celine had been afraid this was going to happen, what with the way her blood levels had fluctuated up and down over the last few weeks. But she'd been hoping things would return to normal once she'd finished radiation. Unfortunately, they hadn't.

"Your nurses will be in to get you prepped," the doctor said, "and please don't worry. You'll be feeling a lot better very soon."

"Thank you, Doctor," Celine said, but when he left, she looked at Lauren and tears filled her eyes. "What am I going to do? I haven't had medical insurance in five weeks, and bills are already coming in left and right."

Lauren held Celine's hand.

Celine swallowed hard. "As it is, I'm going to have to use all my savings to pay the bills I incurred over the last month, and I'll have to use one of my credit cards to make a pretty large down payment for this transfusion. But if I do that, I won't be able to pay our mortgage next month because all my cards will be maxed out. I'll also have to pull Kassie out of Mitchell Prep. She'll have to go to public school because we just don't have that kind of money anymore."

Lauren shook her head with sadness. "Keith should be ashamed of himself. And has he still not even called Kassie?"

"No, not since the day after she heard that woman on the phone. She was so devastated behind all that, but thank God her therapist is really helping her cope with everything. Still, I've got to figure out where we're going to live, and sick or not, I've got to get back to work before I lose all my clients. Dear Lord, how did all this happen?" she said, covering her eyes with both hands.

Lauren pulled Celine's hands away from her face. "Look, enough is enough. I know you're never going to ask, so I'm going to handle things the way I see fit. Kassie's already been through enough, so taking her out of her school and away from her friends won't be good. But more important, you and I both know that even though you're cancer free, you can't continue stressing over bills or anything else. Stress is the worst thing in the world for you right now...so this is what we're going to do. I'm going to take out a second mortgage on my house, pay for your transfusion and hospital stay, pay Kassie's tuition for both this semester and next, and when you're feeling better, we're going to place your house on the market. We're then going to pack up all your things, put most of it in storage, and you and Kassie are going to move in with me until you get back on your feet."

Celine raised her eyebrows and shook her head, disagreeing. "No, that's way too much. I could never do that. I appreciate the offer, but—"

"But nothing," Lauren said matter-of-factly. "This isn't something open for discussion. I'm doing what I have to do, and what I know God wants me to do."

"But—"

Lauren folded her arms and leaned back in her chair. "This conversation is over. I won't let you die because of stress or money. I just won't."

Tears streamed down Celine's face, and Lauren got up and hugged her. They held each other closely, and although they were best friends forever and had been for years, somehow their friendship felt stronger—at this very moment. They were sisters with different parents, but they were sisters for life. Lauren had proven that today more than ever before, and Celine would give her life for Lauren if it became necessary. She loved and cherished this woman who was doing the unthinkable—a woman who was making an incredible sacrifice. The kind of sacrifice most blood relatives wouldn't as much as consider making for their own kin.

But this gesture on Lauren's part confirmed that she was the wonderful person Celine had always known her to be: a great woman of God with true integrity. She was going to be the perfect wife for Jackson, and Celine thanked God for Lauren. She thanked God for His mercy, His grace, and His peace. She thanked Him for His unwavering love—she thanked Him for absolutely everything.

Acknowledgments

To my Heavenly Father, thank you for absolutely everything. To my dear husband, Will, for more than I can say. You have been the love of my life for twenty-five amazing years, and I thank God for you daily. I love you mind, body, and soul, eternally. To my brothers, Willie, Jr., and Michael (and Marilyn) Stapleton—no matter how old we get, you are both still my "little" brothers who I will forever love with all my heart. I thank God for both of you. To my stepson and daughter-in-law, Trenod and Tasha Vines-Roby, our grandchildren, Alex (Lamont) and Trenod, Jr., and to the rest of my family (Tennins, Ballards, Lawsons, Stapletons, Youngs, Beasleys, Haleys, Romes, Greens, Robys, Garys, Shannons, and Normans): I love you all.

To my dear cousin and fellow author, Patricia Haley-Glass (and Jeffrey), my dear best friends, Kelli Tunson Bullard and Lori Whitaker Thurman, my dear cousin, Janell Green, my loving spiritual mom, Dr. Betty Price, and my spiritual sisters (the Price daughters), Angela Evans, Cheryl Price, and Stephanie Buchanan: I love each and every one of you so very much.

Acknowledgments

To my attorneys, Ken Norwick and J. Stephen Sheppard, my hugely supportive and amazing publisher, Hachette/Grand Central Publishing—Beth de Guzman, Linda Duggins, Jamie Raab, Elizabeth Connor, Caroline Acebo, Maddie Caldwell, Stephanie Serabian, the entire sales and marketing teams, along with everyone else at GCP, and to my talented freelance team: Connie Dettman, Luke LeFevre, Pamela Walker-Williams, and Ella Curry—thank you all for everything!

To four of my fellow authors who continue to support me, year after year, who are also great friends: Trice Hickman, Eric Jerome Dickey, Trisha Thomas, and Marissa Monteilh—thank you. To all the bookstores and retailers who sell my books, every media organization, website or blog that promotes them, and to all the fabulous book clubs that select my novels for their monthly discussions—thanks a million and then some.

To the truly kind people who make my writing career possible: my readers. **You are, by far, the best readers in the whole wide world, and I am beyond grateful.**

Much love and God bless you always,

Kimberla Lawson Roby

E-mail: kim@kimroby.com
Facebook: www.facebook.com/kimberlalawsonroby
Twitter: @KimberlaLRoby
Instagram: www.instagram.com/kimberlalawsonroby
Periscope: @kimberlalawsonroby

Reading Group Guide

1. At the start of the book Celine has spent the last five years building her career. Do you think it is important that women are able to focus on their careers as much as men? How do you balance work and home life? Do you think Celine manages to do this successfully?

2. When Celine first feels a lump in her breast, she doesn't tell anyone and goes to the doctor alone. Why do you think she doesn't want to tell her family and friends? Does this make the diagnosis process more difficult for her?

3. Keith claims that Celine was too focused on her work and not paying enough attention to him. Do you think she should have noticed that he was distant and unhappy? Was Keith effective in how he communicated that to Celine? Have you ever

missed signs of a deteriorating relationship? If so, please explain.

4. Lauren steps in to take care of Celine when she needs it most. Do you have best friends that you can count on like this? If so, please share your experience. Is this type of relationship uniquely female? How do you think male friendship differs from female friendship?

5. Celine's doctors and nurses stress the importance of giving yourself breast exams and getting regular mammograms. Do you and your loved ones take these precautions? Have you, a loved one, or a close friend been personally affected by breast cancer? Do you think that there is enough awareness about how to detect breast cancer early?

6. Were you surprised by the way Keith reacted to Celine's diagnosis? If so, why? Was there a time in your life when someone really let you down?

7. Kassie has a very difficult time with Keith's decision to leave. How does her behavior change once her father is gone? Do you think she blames Celine? If so, why?

8. Celine struggles with the challenges of a cancer diagnosis and her marriage falling apart, and her

emotions are very up and down. How does Lauren bring her out of these dark places? How does Celine reconcile her hard times with her relationship to God?

9. Do you agree with Celine's decision to let Keith come back? Lauren and Jackson are very against the idea. Are there times when you have made a decision that your family and friends didn't support? Should married couples consider the opinions of others when trying to work out their marital differences? Why or why not?

10. How do the events of the book change Celine's relationship with Kassie? Do you think they have become closer? Do you think Kassie will eventually come to terms with her father's betrayal?

11. In the end, Lauren makes a huge sacrifice for Celine and Kassie because "they were sisters with different parents, but they were sisters for life." Do you have friends that have become more like family to you?